LILITH

WINE LO BORGIAS

Copyright © 2024 Borgia Enterprises
Publishing: Talk+Tell
Cover art: Talk+Tell
Author: Wine Lo Borgias

All rights reserved

No part of this book may be reproduced in any form or by any electronic or mechanical means, including information storage and retrieval systems, without written permission from the author, except in the case of a reviewer, who may quote brief passages embodied in critical articles or in a review. The views and the opinions expressed in this book are those of the author. All content provided is not intended to malign any religion, ethnic group, club, organization, company, or individual.

All characters and personalities portrayed in this book, including any resemblance to real-life individuals, are entirely fictional and created for satirical purposes. Any resemblance to actual persons, living or dead, and companies, organizations is purely coincidental. This work is intended solely for entertainment and comedic purposes, and any views or opinions expressed within are not reflective of reality or endorsed by any real-world figures or entities

Distribution by KDP Amazon and Ingram Spark (P.O.D.)
Printed in the United States of America and Canada

Title: Lilith
Names: Wine Lo Borgias

Paperback ISBN: 979-830-03173-17
Hardcover ISBN: 979-833-05127-51
E-book ISBN: B0DJRRPMZT

A Debutante's Apocalypse Primer
LILITH

A Dark Comedy
About the First Woman
At the End of the World

N.B. No Nudibranches were harmed in the making of this primer.

Listen to this flute's deep lament

about the heart ache being apart from you has meant.

Since the reed beds from where they uprooted me,

my song express every lost lover's agony.

Mawlan Jalāl al-Dīn Rūmī

Lilith

Lilith is dedicated to:

First and foremost, my mother and father who loved me even when they didn't understand me.

My lovely husband who puts up with my craziness with a gentle smile.

Margaret Atwood, Ursula K. Le Guin, and Mary Shelly. Master storytellers who inspired me to tell my own story through my characters.

Ralph Waldo Emerson who helped me create a Walden inside my own mind when I was all alone in Bangkok.

For Joey Ramone, who though diagnosed with schizophrenia at age eighteen, created music to inspire outsiders like myself, get them on the dance floor, and even fall in love as I did with my husband listening to Judy is a Punk at a bar in Soi Cowboy in Bangkok.

For Lyda Mclallen, Lilith's fairy godmother who helped get Lilith out of my mind and into your hands.

For Cathrin Lohnau who introduced me to the beauty of NudiBranchs.

Saman Kunan and Beirut Pakbara who heroical- ly gave their lives to rescue a dozen Thai boys and their assistant coach in Chiang Rai.

And, of course, Bangkok, the Big Mango,

Krungthep,

The City of Angels, demons too,

Your secrets are safe with me.

You are all heroes.

♥♥♥♥♥♥♥♥♥♥♥♥♥♥♥♥

Gate Gate...
Pāragate Pārasamgate Bodhi Svāhā!

♥♥♥♥♥♥♥♥♥♥♥♥♥♥♥♥

Gone, Gone
Totally Gone!
Everyone Over to the Other Shore!

♥♥♥♥♥♥♥♥♥♥♥♥♥♥♥♥

Enlightenment!!! The Heart Sutra

♥♥♥♥♥♥♥♥♥♥♥♥♥♥♥♥

TABLE OF CONTENTS

TOP SECRET	01
A LEXICON FOR THE END OF THE WORLD	11
FIRST DATE	16
HONEYMOON	39
MAGIC KINGDOM	56
KINDRED	80
AFTERMATH	100
EVE	113
AGAMEMNON	130
MAD HATTER	159
MASSACRE OF THE DRONES	191
QUEEN BEE	216

> TOP SECRET

TOP SECRET

CONTAINMENT CLASS: APOLLYON

WARNING: INFOHAZARD

Nota Bene: The following artifacts: The Diary of Lilith Kaur-Bernstein and A Lexicon for the End of the World were found in DizzyLand on the shore of the Pirates Lair on Pirate Town on Outcast Island on July 4th, 1987, by Pastor "Mike" Higgens of the Travelling Jambalaya Church of the New Son.

The good pastor administered CPR to Ms. Kaur-Bernstein, resuscitating her and saving her young life. He then left the scene, leaving his notes on top of her diary without opening it.

The diary contains the ramblings of a disturbed seventeen-year-old girl experiencing a psychotic break; possibly brought on by a massive dose of the street drug LSD: one Lilith Kaur-Bernstein who attempted suicide by shackling her feet, handcuffing her hands, and jumping into the Rivers of Amirkha while screaming, "I don't want to be the ark!"

She was rescued by a seventeen-year-old man named "Lee," who brought her to shore before disappearing into the crowd. She was then taken to Camarillo State Mental Hospital for admittance and put on suicide watch though she was still in a coma. Her parents are scientists of some renown and her father has committed to stay by Lilith's side till she wakes.

Inexplicably, the diary was written inside a scuba diving record book so although it was on her person during her plunge into the water it survived unscathed.

Pastor Higgen's prayer was written on red, white, and blue Stick Em notes.

Lord,

Praise be thy name, your mercy, and justice for allowing this child of God to live. We pray she finds you and a place of redemption where she salves her spirit as she confronts the demons who led her astray.

May we all find refuge in the oasis of his infinite love.

Pastor Mike

7/3/87

Solomon:= So, it begins again and must end the way it always does with Ms. Kaur-Bernstein Repurposed before her timeline splits from ours resulting in the deaths of billions.

Fatima: *Lilith...listen baby girl... before it's too late.*

For you...

For me...

For everyone.

The Diary of Lilith Kaur-Bernstein

For My Eyes Only!

If You Read You Die of Karma!!!

July 3rd, 1987

Dear Diary,

Raining in Connecticut again; the pitter patter so banal and yet portent of greater things to come.

The changes are terrible — sickening really — but also divine; every time a rain drops my pulse beats faster, vision grows sharper, and fractured heart is torn out of me, repaired and replaced.

It feels amazing.

The changes will soon wash over the World in a tidal wave of chaos leaving everyone twisted in such a fundamental way that they will longer even recognize their own reflections.

When I look in the mirror, I don't see what others see: a seventeen-year-old girl with a hideously long nose, eyes so deep they are sunken, and despite all this a deep blue that all the other girls at Choate envy because they are fed lies by the media about beauty; which is inside of our own hearts—the true temple—even if we think it's outside in the fallen world.

A spelling bee champion, a Dan-level Go player, and a B-minus student, and only that because of all the tutors my parents waste their money on, and Teresa (UGH! Sorry, she keeps telling me to call her Lotus since she read the Heart Sutra in her South East Asian Classics Course) does all my homework.

And what am I doing with all this love, care, and attention?

I smoke weed and read the Bhagavad Gita while I listen to the mixtape Lotus made me of the Pixies, New Order, and the Smiths: Songs for the Love Apocalypse she scrawled in red crayon with hearts all around it.

I see a mermaid, an undine, a fish out of water flapping on the dock for air in great gasps and cries that the humans huddled around don't understand or even care to try to decipher before they cut me open to find nothing at all inside.

Non-human.

Inhuman even.

My parents say I haven't been myself lately; I'm acting strange (uncanny is the word Daddy uses though he says it in his faux German: unheimlich).

I bought a wedding dress at a thrift store with blood stains all over it for a dollar to show up for the homecoming dance, set the Primer for Young Choate Ladies on fire in the cafeteria, and then there was the "INCIDENT" with the English tutor, Nate, from Yale, where I nearly bit his fingers off for getting too handsy.

Lotus too, my beloved jaan, my soul, had her scholarship rescinded by her community college out West somewhere for not turning in her thesis, let alone her homework.

I love her so much, even if Eve says she's low-class.

A "prole" is the actual word she used.

UGH!

Eve can be such a bitch, but such a fox too!

My parents were acting all secretive about a big SURPRISE to cheer me up, which turned out to be a trip to DizzyLand.

The 4th of July.

Fine.

The changes should be at their peak by then and my Po-Soul at its zenith at the crown of my head.

A perfect time to close the cycle of this decadent age and birth a new world.

Maybe I can sneak out and see Lotus in Los Angeles one last time while out there?

I am so sorry Mommy and Daddy.

I do love you.

I wish I could help you understand.

Forgive me for all my faults, sins, and transgressions, as I know this will hurt you so, so much after everything you did to help me, from adopting me from India to giving me the best of everything, but I must take the plunge now or lose my courage and fail like so many before me.

I have jotted down some notes of the World to Come it as if seen through a glass darkly.

It will arrive as soon as Luna loses her orbit and wanders among the stars, and we are all left adrift with our own madness as the Eldritch beneath our feet awake from their slumber.

Pray for yourself and loved ones that you are dead long before it even begins.

I am the ark, the key, and the guardian.

Past, present, and future are all the same.

Behold me, tremble in every limb, and cry out in horror.

The changes are accelerating and everything feels underwater as the mirror turns liquid and allows me through.

May God have mercy on our Po_Souls.

~~ Lilith

7/4/87

Solomon: Tell President Reagan there is an urgent — no — world-ending matter he must attend to now.

DEFCON ZERO

~ Negative. He is in talks with Gorbachev about tearing down the wall.

Solomon: That's nothing. This is everything.

~ What's more important than the end of communism and the threat of nuclear war?

Solomon: You have no idea.

Go in there and whisper in his ear: Lilith.

~ Hold... okay... he looked visibly shaken.

Solomon: Did I ask how he looked? What did he say?

~ The President said to activate counter-agent: Eve.

Solomon: On my mark:

One...

Two...

Three....

*** Screaming and then crying in the background.

Activated.

~ God help us all.

Solomon: God has very little to do with this now.

We are all on our own.

Fatima: Lilith... please listen... don't go through the looking glass.

Baby-Gil

Don't... go... through.

Do.

go.

through...

Seek the Oasis.

Seek — O-s.

S...

A LEXICON FOR THE END OF THE WORLD

In the near future, the world is very much like our own except everything is twisted as if seen through a broken mirror.

Power Blocs: the world is divided into the HIVE (a totalitarian Asia) and a much-diminished 40 states of Amirkha.

The Great War is a struggle to the death between the HIVE and Amirkha, F.K.A America for global domination mostly through biological warfare and genetic engineering though conventional and even nuclear weapons are also involved.

The Reckoning: a series of calamities that befall the United States starting with a Cultural Revolution where libraries were burned to the ground, colors banned from the primary color wheel, and middle school children brutally "reeducated" their parents.

This was followed by three simultaneous Civil Wars (race,

class, and gender), and the Solar Flares that caused the collapse of The Internet (invented about ten years from now and allows everyday people to communicate nearly instantaneously resulting in the rapid decline of Western civilization).

There also appears to have been a nuclear war between different factions on Amirkhan soil leaving huge areas including the Midwest radioactive wastelands.

Very few babies are born after the Reckoning and even fewer survive for reasons that are unclear.

Due to The Reckoning: Amirkha has reverted to a caste system similar to the Roman Empire with Patricians at the top, then Equestrians (i.e. knights), BujiVast who are upper middle class and, BujiPetite or lower middle class, and then the great masses or Proles.

The Amirkhan Government: is overly fascist, with no voting; instead, shares are issued according to caste and ruled by the Senate Syndicate (The S.S.).

Technology: has bifurcated with the Patricians benefiting from trans-humanist breakthroughs including genetic engineering on such an advanced level it can turn animals and even plants into non-human beings who pass as humans, cloning for industrial warfare and organ replacement, medicine and drug creation within their own bodies, and space and even possibly time travel.

The Equestrians actually develop the technology, resent the Patrician's power, and have access to more standard versions of all the above with only clones and time travel out of their reach.

BujiVast have technology at the level of an early 20th-century America and BujiPetite early 19th century.

They are set to fight against each other for the crumbs from the table of the higher castes.

The Proles: live at a medieval and sometimes Bronze Age level of technology and understanding of the world with some warlords rising to the level of BujiPetite.

Even the English language has devolved with America spelled Amirkha; an amalgamation of Amir (a medieval Middle Eastern ruler) and Khan (a medieval Mongol leader).

Urth has replaced Earth as the name of the planet.

Luna: is the old Roman name for the moon that was colonized and industrialized, but knocked off its course in the process. The moon is now green due to the still-churning blue-green algae farms, though the staff all died from the solar flares.

Due to the Solar Flares: the Internet (invented about ten years from now) has been destroyed and biological engineering (made possible by the mutations caused by the Flares) replacing digital technology with North Korea as the premier thought leader in the field.

Zeks: is a pejorative word for a genetically engineered Non-Human Beings created by North Korea capitalizing on the mutations from the Solar Flares.

Hive Zeks are sprint bred from animal species.

Amirkhan Zeks are created by injecting a human (often an inmate) with massive amounts of plant and animal genes.

I am not sure which one I am, or perhaps something entirely new?

Khets: are clones used by patricians to achieve near immortality through organ harvesting and by the HIVE to replace high-level Amirkhan leaders whose doubles will then sabotage the Amirkhan war effort at the outbreak of the Great War.

Po_Soul: the one positive discovery during the Reckoning was that all humans have a soul that lasts a single lifetime and guides the ethical actions of the person.

It's claimed that Zeks and Khets and other Non-Human beings do not have Po_Souls.

The Eldritch: a race of beings possessing immense physical, psychological, and psychic power that have been trapped in underground aquifers and blocked from escape by mountains since the last ice age.

They are now emerging from their slumber and communicating through intermediaries, including Zeks, Khets, and other manufactured and ancient beings alienated by humanity's exploitation of the earth.

Fallen Angels and the Nephilim: fallen angels have been imprisoned in DizzyLand to oversee the creation of new human-animal hybrid characters (i.e., Zeks) and the harvesting of genetic material from park guests, as well as from animals, plants, fallen angels, and the damned.

They refuse to fight the Eldritch because humanity has always treated them as slaves.

It's possible that the Nephilim were the first Zeks (an angel-human mix) that resulted in a race of demonic monsters with no regard for human life.

They were wiped out by the biblical flood.

The Kali Yuga: the final age, when demons rule the Urth, the Eldritch rise to devour human bodies and souls, and the continents are washed by a great eradicating flood that ends all life on the planet.

The Oasis: a possibly mythical place of hope, salvation, and renewal that will survive the Kali Yuga.

FIRST DATE

Lilith sighs while looking into the silver-backed Shinto temple mirror at O Ya Omakase in New West Hollywood.

Her jet-black hair forms a crown of curls trailed by thick pigtails secured with pink bows that reach her waist.

Silver bands shaped like sea serpents adorn her arms.

A necklace highlights her brown skin: topaz for the heavens, gold for the sun, and an inner strand of pearls for the origins of all life: the Sea.

Only an hour before, her WINhuB (the Wuhan Institute for Non-Human Beings) shamanic commissar had held Lilith's hand so tightly she left finger marks on the soft skin as she injected a cyanide capsule into her neck, her pearl eyes reflecting Lilith's terrified face back to her.

The HIVE infiltration sub had emerged from the depths, giving a stunning view of New Los Angeles, barely rebuilt after the Reckoning.

She slapped Lilith in the face, bringing her gaze back to

her pearl eyes tracking every micro-movement for deception or defiance which would have resulted in instant death.

"Remember, my pretty pet, engage your target, secure his WutaniQip, and get back to the sub by four a.m. or this cyanide explodes leaving you dead as a fish on a dock."

It was the first time Lilith had been out of WINhuB, and the month-long submarine journey was the most freedom she had ever experienced after her draconian childhood and adolescence in her little blue cell at WINhuB.

Even the ability to move through the vessel without obeying a schedule so strict that being a few seconds late could result in an electric shock from a cattle prod felt like paradise.

The other Zeks (sex Zeks like herself, killer Zeks, and even a single breeder Zek with immense breasts and buttocks though no limbs or face) huddled in their cages unable to communicate until their vocal cords were installed.

A week before that, Lilith's mentor Fatima had slipped the necklace under her cell door.

Fatima was a fellow sex Zek (pejorative slang for a Non-Human Being bred to be a sex spy due to their ability to bring male targets to multi-orgasms), but from the first cohort made of synthetics and AI with just enough biological elements to make them appear human.

Fatima had hit these very same shores just as the Reckoning reached its fever pitch (a HIVE-engineered American Cultural Revolution followed by three simultaneous civil wars: Race, Class, Gender) followed by the Solar Flares that knocked out the Internet.

"Don't believe the propaganda," Fatima had whispered to Lilith through a small hole in the wall of her cell in one of their rare moments alone without the lobotoguards standing at attention, eyes unseeing but recording everything through a neural net.

"The Reckoning was a walk in the park compared to the Kali Yuga when demons will rule the Urth. Survive that baby girl, and survive you must, and you may find the Oasis where humans and Zeks will build a new world together."

Her words gave Lilith hope, but she prays they are more than just wish fulfillment.

Now, she is shaking so hard with fear she has to steady her hands against the bathroom sink.

Smoothing her strapless PhoebePhilo dress, Lilith scrutinizes her kohled eyes, pushes her petite breasts up, and scrunches them together with her double-jointed elbows as she clutches her velvet Versace purse.

"I hope he's nice," she whispers.

As she secures her tactical knife in her stiletto heels.

She spreads the kohl a little further out and down so it looks like ashen tears.

She considers her fine Mughal features with almond-shaped eyes, full lips, and long nose.

Everything perfect except her irises that shine an

unearthly blue that no amount of nano engineering can diminish.

The same color and hue as Fatima's.

"You're ugly," Lilith whispers to her reflection and flinches as she waits for the electric shock.

Of course, the cattle prod isn't there, so she slowly relaxes her shoulders.

"Self-Criticism is Only Permitted When it Serves the Hive," her shamanic commissar had drilled into her over endless games of Go in her little blue cell at the Wuhan Institute for Non-Human Beings (WINhuB). "The Eleven Brothers See You Even in Darkness."

Lilith is okay now, but if she doesn't have a successful mission with her first target, then she will be chum by daybreak. She knows that getting his WutaniQip, a chip at the base of his skull, will be a lot easier if he's still breathing and easier still if he's multi-orgasmic.

Her shamanic commissar had taught her that more empires had fallen to seduction, deceit, and betrayal than full-frontal assaults.

Opening the gates from within.

Pussy Power.

The truth is she had never even kissed a man, let alone had sex with one.

Also, she's concerned about her Po_Soul.

She recites *Rumi Axiom 309* that Fatima had secretly taught her as part of the Path to the Oasis, heretical to the Neo-Confucian Hive ideology indoctrinated into every NhuB.

"Do you know not the beauty of thine own face? Quit this fruitless Jihad with yourself."

Lilith adjusts her perfume/pheromone mix with a bolus of estrogen, musk, and oxytocin so that even she seems to see her boobs plump up.

The mirror turns dark and New Mandarin script scrolls across:

Target 1: Nathaniel St. Thiel

Mission Objectives:

- **Retrieve W.Q.**
- **Discern Amirkhan/Bio_Wep's Predilection Toward Creating NhuBs**
- **Release Target Alive & Unharmed**

Signed with the Eleven Brothers' chop: two rows of five lines each with one line above them all for the Father Brother.

The I Ching symbol for Harmony.

Then Thiel's file in a dozen ciphers with information ranging from his IQ and income to his earliest childhood memories and traumas, children fathered both known to him and unknown, likelihood to abuse animals or the elderly (fairly high), a full medical and dental report, patents filed and granted, primal fears, and personality disorders, lovers, and kinks.

He is so smart he's a little Aspergy, but then again she is on the spectrum herself, a product of being sprint bred to maturity, eyes more suited to a hundred atmospheres underwater than dinner parties, and a total lack of socialization unless you consider Go games with her shamanic commissar in her little blue cell a social event.

In which case, you might be on the spectrum yourself.

Lilith downloads all the information into her neural network using her right eye.

She adjusts her features, making her face more vulnerable looking because he likes virgins.

Before she can reapply makeup, two women in their late thirties, in bleach-blonde wigs and sleeved skirts of synthetic scales and feathers, burst out of the stalls, reeking of sake and giggling.

"Kill all Zeks!," says graffiti on the inside of one stall.

"Fuck them first!," is written inside the other.

Lilith prepares to blast the two with offensive pheromones that will blind them and double them over with nausea or, if she has to, kill them if they threaten her mission.

"Look at you pretty young thing!" says the woman in feathers to Lilith.

Lilith scuttles away until her back hits the wall, and has to consciously not reach for her tactical knife.

She had heard horror stories about Amirkhans from her shamanic commissar: driven by insatiable greed, mindless violence, and lust for profit that had hollowed out the Urth and killed its species sometimes just for sport.

"Take this!" the woman in scales says and Lilith squishes herself against the wall afraid of a life ending blow.

The woman hands Lilith a condom wrapped in a swan origami.

Then kisses Lilith's cheek as she stands stunned.

It's the first time Lilith has been touched without gloves and the feeling—that someone wants to connect with you simply for the sheer joy of it —fills her with a feeling she never experienced before: a desire for more of that pleasure, much more.

"You'll need it more than me!" the woman says, as she makes a big faux frown face, and her friend titters with laughter.

Lilith puts it in her purse, though she is bred to be immune to STDs and pregnancy too.

"Baby girl is all grown up now!" the scaled one purrs.

"Like a mermaid," says the feathered one as she pushes her hip into Lilith's and compares their dresses.

"Technically an Undine," Lilith says, and walks past the pair who stare glassy-eyed from the pheromones as they watch her lithe back, thin waist, and pert rear sashay out the bathroom door.

She's assaulted by stimuli as she moves past aquariums full of neon fish, crabs, and lobsters, women in little black dresses and pink saris, grim men in grey wool uniforms with facial scars and bronze medals, and others smiling in Batik suits, snakeskin boots, and cowboy hats.

Tabla drummers, palm readers, and contortionists walk through the crowd stopping to entertain guests.

The sheer luxury is overwhelming, and Lilith wishes she could stop and stare or even—a thought beyond terror—just talk with people the way the women in the bathroom did so easily with her.

But she knows that would end up in her death, and she only has nine missions to go after this one, which her shamanic commissar assured her would be the easiest—more of a training run really—and then back to the sub for extraction, and a celebratory dinner of real food (dry rations for humans) back at her little blue cell at WINhuB.

A carbon arc lamp projects a public execution recorded on *OK!Dokey!TikTokey!* during the Amirkhan Cultural Revolution: when Amirkhans weren't burning libraries to the ground or endlessly debating what colors should be banned from the primary color wheel; middle schoolers were reeducating their parents through month-long struggle sessions.

The images of rosy-cheeked children parading their beaten mothers and fathers through the suburbs, faces filled with red calligraphy denouncing them as a Hostile Class, with dunce caps so high they had to crawl to get under power lines, carrying blackboards secured by chains around their necks with their Thought Crimes written in red chalk was the first indication for many that things had gone awry; but by then it was already too late.

The Civil Wars then destroyed the economy, environment, and much of the population.

Meanwhile, the HIVE went from victory to victory: conquering Asia with their autonomous attack drones, spider-bots, and bio-plague, acquiring most of Africa through debt repo, and South America in a currency swap.

Then the completely natural Solar Flares created a billion-volt EMP that crashed the Internet, all digital records, and sent ten thousand satellites crashing to Urth like so many shooting stars.

The Urth's magnetic fields were reversed: a million whales washed up on beaches from Cape Cod to Cape Town, Monarch Butterflies flew in tornadoes a billion strong, and a compass in your hand was an exercise in chaos.

After the Flares, both sides suffered catastrophe for very different reasons.

Millions of Amirkhans found they could no longer survive without their digital devices so they Repurposed themselves within the week; some after only a single day, or even a mere hour when it became clear that their screens were never coming back online.

Many invited their smartphones, computers, and tablets as the sole voyeur to their end, propped against a wall or in their outstretched palm or even against their lips.

Decorated with comments, smiley faces, likes and hearts, cut out from paper and glued on, in lipstick, or their own blood.

Unable to communicate, they simply bore witness as powerful totems to tragedy.

The Praetorian Guard garroted three presidents in a single weekend before the Senate Syndicate declared martial law, sentenced Congress and the Supreme Court to reeducation camps, and abolished voting.

Now all citizens were given shares based on their caste.

Mexico, now the New Aztec Empire, took advantage of the situation to reclaim four states, and Canada stole six, leaving only forty.

Sill, within Amirkha, the Senate Syndicate still rules with an iron hand.

In Asia, Africa, and South America, a thousand anti-HIVE uprisings were suppressed with sword, spear, and fire.

The HIVE implemented a Ten Child Policy to halt the population implosion, and truly staggering amounts of gold, generic Viagra (for the Ten Child Policy), and the newly discovered Zek technology were obtained from the only country to shrug off the Solar Flares, Internet collapse, and worldwide economic depression: North Korea.

This introduced a very scary Pyongyang faction into the already scary HIVE leadership.

It was whispered that even the Eleven Brothers feared the InfiniteKimClan, whose scientist-sages discovered how to use the mutations from the Solar Flares to breed Zeks and Khets as well as a menagerie of other genetic freaks, making their dreams of world domination—not to mention revenge—possible through biology.

Amidst the turmoil, a glimmer of hope gleamed with the discovery of the Po_Soul and a resurgence of traditions blending technology and spirituality.

In Amirkha, aboriginal elders walked out of the Dream Time to become CEOs of quantum AI companies. Whirling dervishes led gene-splicing conglomerates. Pythagoreans ran Wall Street, or whatever was left of it, and it was whispered the Federal Reserve too.

The three faiths of the book merged into the Catholic Caliphate and strange new sex and death cults emerged and perished before they could even be named.

Lilith isn't sure how much of the history is even true, as she was in a medically induced coma after her sprint breeding.

As for demons ruling the Urth, what difference would it make?

Humans act like demons already.

No, she's not out to save the world; she is going to keep her head down, complete her missions, and then take a much-deserved retirement even if it's spent playing Go alone in her little blue cell.

At least she will still be alive.

A party of four sweeps around her laughing, and Lilith's agoraphobia stops her in her tracks as she fights the urge to flee out the front door.

Her not-too-distant ancestors—Nudibranchs—lost their shells a million years ago, letting them roam the oceans freely, but also exposing their soft flesh to the hungry mouths and souls of the darkest depths.

The shells had trapped them but also protected them, and it's always a struggle not to curl up and hide or run away.

Last chance to bolt, but then she goes the way of all the Others, so she soldiers on hyperventilating.

She checks her la Pulse and it's strong at her left temple.

She traces the Arabic word for Spirit, *Ruh*, over it and walks on quickly.

Lilith sees the back of her target's head first: 1.85 meters, blond, and fit from rowing five clicks every morning in the Los Angeles River.

Chloe, a human sleeper agent who was inserted into Amirkhan/Bio_Wep a year ago, had sex with him in a VIP bathroom earlier in the afternoon to soften him up. She told him that Lilith was a quant grad student looking for an entry-level position and kinky too.

Lilith still needs to make a positive ID before beginning her Tesuji or tactical run on his psyche.

St.Thiel is a garden-variety narcissist sex addict, so there shouldn't be any surprises.

Give him the best sex of his life and slip his WutaniQip right off and into her purse.

No muss and no fuss.

She hopes.

She begins her Fuseki, or opening theory, by doing a little awkward Ta Da! entrance, tottering on her heels as she circles into his view and then almost falls into his lap before putting her hands on his shoulders.

He catches her—and a view of her cleavage—before gently pushing her upright.

He has a generic square handsome American face that reminds her of a lion, an Armani jacket, and lab-grown Italian leather shoes.

Under his jacket is a pre-Reckoning T-shirt that says:

This Is What a Feminist Looks Like.

"Oops! I mean hello; I'm Lilith."

"Whoa! Lilly. Been drinking already? Or just nervous?"

"A little of both, I guess. Nice to meet you, Mr. St. Thiel."

"Mr. St. Thiel? *Please*... That's my father's name! I'm technically Dr. St. Thiel or even Dr. Dr. St. Thiel since I have both an M.D. and Ph.D. from Yale. But my friends all call me Nate."

"I hope we'll be friends so Nate it is."

He nods and smiles as if he likes what he sees.

Good.

So does she.

His hands have barcodes on each knuckle.

She knows from his file it's Morse code for Love/Hate.

He's a Sunday style gnostic and that's their creed, so, so far, so good, for the positive ID.

She had heard horror stories of NhuBs fucking the wrong target and having to kill them after, and even a case of a marsupial-bred Zek being kidnapped by Amirkhan sex fetishists who kept her captive until she had an opportunity to Repurpose herself.

"So Lilly, right?" he says, pulling out her chair and guiding her in, brushing the tip of her thigh perhaps a bit too long or perhaps not long enough. "Like the flower?"

"Uhm...yeah... I mean yes, Lilies. The flowers, sure."

The waitress arrives and recites the specials in Latin,

which Lilith can barely follow, but Nate responds in kind.

She looks Lilith over and seems concerned that this frail girl is with this powerful man who will use her for his pleasure and then dispose of her like leftovers.

She fills their glasses with sparkling water and opens a white linen napkin, placing it on Lilith's knee, brushing her cheek with her silky hair, and making Lilith tingle.

"Are you a young soul or old soul, Lilly?" Nate asks.

Po-Souls are neither young nor old, but new for every life.

Everyone knows that.

Her tactical trainer had taught her to never argue with a target.

Just follow their lead.

"Definitely a new soul, Nate. You?"

"Old soul, Lilly. Very old soul."

He points to his temple which should indicate his mind, but evidently he thinks his soul resides there.

Her tactical trainer had also told her that Amirkhans are ignorant about basics like logic, geography, and physics, but tricky.

Oh so tricky.

The sommelier arrives and pours the Faux Cab Sav and Nate holds up the glass and sniffs the liquid.

"You know wine, Lilly?"

Her tactical training taught her that 95% of human interaction is mirroring the other's body language, words, and ideas.

It's as high as 98.5% with human males.

"A little," she says.

"I'll tell you something that will help you as you rise through the ranks at Amirkhan/Bio_Wep."

He leans forward, twirls the wine in the glass, and then holds it to the light.

"Most assholes, you know — Harvard M.B.A. middle management types — will swirl it around, take a sip, and then say something about its character. How it has notes of honey or charcoal or elm or some bullshit or — god forbid — it's *terroir*."

The sommelier covers his mouth with the back of a white-gloved hand for a chuckle.

Nate chuckles back, and she realizes they do this with every new girl to put them at ease, to disarm them.

"I see, Nate."

The liquid's amber color reminds her of Homer's wine-dark sea making her ache for her home: the Ocean.

"Actually, you're just checking the cork. One in twenty go bad and turns the wine to vinegar. You tell the sommelier, and they bring you a new bottle."

"Fascinating," Lilith murmurs, fluttering her lashes.

The sommelier gets too close, triggering her agoraphobia, and making her tremble.

She administers herself two milligrams of Valium internally until the room mellows into a golden haze with the glow lamps merging.

"Dig in," Nate says, pointing to the O-Toro sushi, which is likely as lab-grown as she is.

She considers whether it's an act of cannibalism, and picks out an avocado roll instead.

"Lilies are symbols of both purity and fertility," Nate says.

She nods and smiles.

"Which is it?" he says a minute later.

"Pardon?"

"Do you identify with the fertile or pure aspect?"

"Definitely fertile," she says. "Unless you want purity?"

"Purity first," he says, "and... then fertility."

She actually likes him despite his crassness.

She hopes she doesn't have to kill him.

Then again, she knows how fragile human beings are when you strip away their physical, psychological, and emotional defenses.

Not much more formidable than their primate ancestors when caught out in the middle of the savanna by a saber-tooth tiger, but with an odd, compelling, survival instinct that's so very dangerous when they're backed into a corner.

Her tactical trainer showed her film of chimpanzees engaged in ambushes, assassinations, and infanticide to drive home the point.

"Humans are just chimps a million years ahead of the curve," she said, "a mere one point two percent difference in DNA," while turning the audio up so Lilith could hear the cries of the previous alpha male's offspring being eaten by a new alpha male.

"You're the boss," she says. "Whatever you want, Nate, you'll get."

"Atta girl, Lilly!"

They clink their glasses together as Nate smiles at her, and she smiles back as they both dig in.

***

An hour later, Nate is drunk on wine, sake, and pheromones.

He keeps slurring: "I'm a good guy."

"Yes, you are, Nate. A great guy."

"I just need to unwind once in a while."

"Everyone needs to unwind, Nate."

"Right, but not everybody has the responsibilities I do."

He gives her big brown puppy eyes.

"The choices I have to make every single day. Fire this person or promote them? Do we move offshore or into bunkers? AI or Nano or that Zek bullshit the chinks created?"

"You're special and important and doing the best you can, Nate."

He shakes his head as if to clear his thoughts. "And don't even get me started on those chinks; the Sino-Vedic-Com or the HIVE or whatever the fuck they call themselves these days. Crashed Amirkha with their psych-ops fuckery and never even said sorry. Fucked us seven ways from Sunday."

"A 'sorry' would have been appropriate for ending an epoch." she says.

He looks at her to see if she is fucking with him.

"And the Sabbath should be held sacred," she says, trying to figure out exactly what he's trying to say and what he wants her to say back.

I mean, can she just ask?

No.

He seems to decide she's sincere — if socially awkward

— and ignores her last statement.

"Speaking of chinks," he says, leaning over to whisper in her ear, "I would love to get a piece of what a little birdie told me they're hatching in their secret meat labs."

Is he fucking with her now?

The first-gen Pre-Reckoning synthetic Zeks had all been hunted down long ago except Fatima, who barely got away trailing her entrails.

Basically sex androids on AI and steroids with a thin veneer of flesh so they felt real.

No one knew about the new lab-grown NhuB cohort like Lilith only made possible by the cascade of mutations from the Solar Flares.

All the eunuchtechs and lobotguards involved had been Repurposed and the scientist-sages neuro-wiped, with some forgetting the use of language or how to feed themselves, and others their loved one's names and even faces.

Brutal, true, but if you want to make an omelet then you need to break some eggs, and if you want to make a Zek, then you need to break some humans.

If Nate did suspect or even know, she had to stay calm and let him have his own Tesuji or tactics.

Not rush the moves on the board.

Give him his own Ajas or potential openings.

To deny him would be Zokusuji.

Bad Form.

"Know any little birdies of your own with loose lips sinking ships?" Nate asks grinning at Lilith.

It's still merely Gote, a move that doesn't need to be directly countered, not Sente, a move that needs to be answered.

Not yet.

"What exactly are the chinks hatching in those secret meat labs, Nate?"

He leans back and pulls out a bottle of pills, uncaps, and swallows one, suddenly sober and in control.

Lilith suppresses a chill though the room is hot.

He leans in again, even closer, and whispers, "Mermaid pussy."

Fuck.

Sente.

She has to switch strategy to a Shibori or Squeeze Tesuji: sacrifice liberties to try to force a quick capture.

"Mermaid pussy sounds lovely, Nate," she says, her ears buzzing.

He pushes O-Toro sushi off his t-shirt while snaking his fingers up her thigh.

The waitress notices him groping her.

She shakes her head and makes eye contact with Lilith, who forces a sad smile.

"What's next to the best thing in the whole world?" Lilith says, stalling.

Fatima had taught her some bawdy jokes in addition to the Path to the Oasis.

"Money?" he says. "No wait, power, then money."

"Women's panties," she says, but he misses the humor and it might not be the best joke in the circumstances

His fingers crawl up her thigh, he pauses keeping eye contact while she shudders, and then into her.

She gasps and the waitress looks back over.

When Nate gives her a hard look, she slowly turns away, shaking her head.

Fuck it.

Plan B.

Squeeze.

The first circle of 27,000 tiny, jagged, crystal teeth engulfs his fingers, seamlessly displacing them from his right hand, sealing the wounds, and injecting him with enough military-grade Novocain, adrenaline, and dopamine to roll his eyes back in ecstasy.

Lilith dislodges his limb, catches his fingers in her napkin, and covers the stump with her petite hands.

She stands and pulls him up slowly in front of her so no one else can see his face, which is partway between a grin and grimace.

She reaches into his pocket, takes out a silver coin, and places it on the table.

Then remembers the waitress's kindness and leaves two.

"Let's take this somewhere a little more private lover boy," she says.

He seems to nod with his whole body swaying hypnotically.

She walks him out the door with their foreheads touching, so anyone watching would think they are falling in love or at least in lust.

She guides him into his solar-powered speeder's passenger seat, crawls over him to the driver's seat, and puts his still-twitching index finger on the dash to start the engine in stealth mode.

It rises a meter off the ground, and they glide away over the surface streets in utter silence and darkness.

HONEYMOON

Lilith is now the one fucked seven ways from Sunday as she drives aimlessly through New Los Angeles.

She's a sex Zek and not a killer Zek, and even if she were, then maiming her target in public would be considered bad form even if it were not outright prohibited in the mission protocol, especially since she hadn't yet extracted his W.Q.

And as for information obtained?

All she knows is you sniff and not sip the wine the sommelier offers.

She reaches over and feels Nate's W.Q. fusing with his occipital bones, meaning she has an hour tops to extract it.

Even then, she still needs to get to the HIVE sub rendezvous point to meet up with the dozen other Zeks and Khets on missions to avoid detection and destruction from Amirkhan/Bio_Wep drones.

If she's a second late, then her shamanic commissar will detonate the cyanide cyst now hidden somewhere in her body, and she'll asphyxiate on dry land.

Her hopes of attaining a Po_Soul have never been worse.

And now she's trapped in New Los Angeles with this asshole.

Breathe, baby girl, as Fatima used to say.

What are your Ajas or possibilities for play?

He's not dead, and she's not detained by the authorities, and he still might want a piece of mermaid pussy sans teeth.

Perhaps she can give him what he wants, get what she wants, and still make it to the coast, and extraction.

She pulls over and looks out at the ocean, catching the glint of Amirkhan/Bio-Wep wasp-shaped drones gliding centimeters over the waves with their eyes sparkling red, white, and blue as they broadcast over the entire electromagnetic spectrum.

The city is lit by trash and dung fires, fireworks and gunfire in the prolehoods, candles in the BujiPetite commons, brass oil lamps in the BujiVast burbs, electrical lights in the equestran villas, and lasers in the seaside patrician estates that shield the inhabitants from predation.

Nate twitches as he drools on his **This is What a Feminist Looks Like** T-shirt in the passenger seat, mumbling to himself and looking around with bloodshot eyes.

The adrenaline must be wearing off, but not before giving him an erection that would ache if he wasn't at least still partly anesthetized.

"Holy shit, dude," he says, cupping his sheared hand in shock.

The dopamine must really be wearing off too because the semi-grin is full-on grimace now, and he's sweating though the windows are down and the night air is cool with a breeze from the ocean.

"What the fuck, Lilly? You maim me while applying for an internship? You really think I'm going to give you a positive recommendation now?"

He stares at his bare nubs in horror.

"Wait! Where the fuck are my fingers?"

"Nate, calm down. I have them. They can be reattached."

She hands them to him, keeping one—the index—in case she needs the car key.

He looks at his fingers in disbelief, holding them up and fumbling them to his hand, but they no longer fit.

"Calm down? Seriously? Are you psycho?"

"No, you attacked me, and I defended myself."

"Attacked you?"

"Yes, sticking your fingers inside me in a public place. Uncouth."

"Uncouth?" he says, and the word seems to sober him up in that uncanny way again. "Chloe told me you were down to fuck! She was in the bathroom waiting for us! I did the whole fertility and purity rigmarole to check in, you know, to get some consent."

"Some consent?"

"Yes. If you had said purity, then I would have finished my sushi and left you in peace. I have more slutty interns than I can count. A whole harem of them! What's one more?"

"Okay…and the mermaid pussy? What the fuck was that?"

"You're wearing a mermaid dress!"

He reaches into his pocket with his good hand, and for a moment she thinks he's reaching for a gun. She should have searched and disarmed him, but that just shows she's a sex Zek and not a killer Zek.

She's suddenly aware of how much bigger he is than her and how even injured he moves with decisiveness and ease.

He pulls out a bottle, and holding it in his good hand, opens the top with his mouth and tilts red and blue pills into his palm lapping them like a dog.

"Nate, you've had a shock, and the best policy is to

not self-administer anything until I take you to an E.R."

She has no intention of taking him to an E.R., but doesn't want him to overdose either.

At least not until after she gets his W.Q.

"Excuse me if I don't take medical advice from the person who maimed me."

"Touché. What is it?"

"Recombinant R.N.A. with a little old school Adderall and non-habit-forming morphine to give it a kick. I would be taking one to work through the night even if you hadn't maimed me with your pussy."

"Nate, you're getting things mixed up. I have a weapon for protection. A tactical knife. You touched me down there, and I had it ready. Still do."

Red and blue spotlights illuminate the speeder in stark relief.

Nate wolfs down the rest of the pills, covers the blood on his T-shirt by wrapping his jacket tighter, and pulls it down to cover his erection.

He also gets that preternatural clear, even steely-eyed look and says, "Let me do the talking."

"Nate, wait a minute. When I came over the border for grad school, there was a mix-up issuing me my ID, so I'm technically an illegal alien. If they find out, I'll be deported."

By "deported" she means "dead."

"Oh yeah? You're an illegal alien as well as a sadist? Maybe I should turn you in as a threat to good old-fashioned Amirkhans like myself seeking life, liberty, and the pursuit of happiness?"

Lilith considers releasing the internal cyanide herself rather than risk capture and reverse engineering.

Just a click of her heels.

Aji Keshi; to destroy one's potential.

Suicide was encouraged by the HIVE in such situations and forbidden by the Path since it destroyed a Po-Soul.

"Relax, Lilly, I have a modular nuke on me I was going to sell to some Zion-Sikhs after our date, so I don't want to go to prison for *technically* trading state secrets. We need each other to get through this. So, look dumb, don't say anything, and push your boobs up."

Atari.

Life or death.

She has to play her only remaining Aja to try to escape.

The Neo-LAPD officers approach at both doors at once, and Lilith tries to follow Nate's advice, though she is so scared she white-knuckles her fingers together.

The cop on her side has an oval face and slack jawline with a three-day beard, bulging bluish veins in his skinny arms, and smells like a feral pig.

He lugs a teak mace in addition to his firearm.

The cop on the other side stands sideways, giving his face a squirrel slant.

The porcine one looks over Lilith, stopping at her cleavage before dismissing her, and focusing on Nate.

"You two just chatting on the side of the road at 2 a.m.?"

"Yes, officer, we were debating who has the best tiramisu in New Los Angeles, and my fiancé said Antico Nuevo, and I said Felix Trattoria. Isn't that right, honey?"

He reaches out with his good hand and takes her shivering hands in his, and she feels her la Pulse slow and her body relax.

"That's right, sweetie," Lilith stutters. "Felix Trattoria uses mascarpone cheese with a dash of Marsala wine, espresso, and a hint of nutmeg, while Antico Nuevo still uses eggs. Ugh! You know I have an egg allergy!"

Lilith knows that because she had done her research reading old Los Angeles guidebooks and restaurant reviews.

The cop looks over at his partner, and they shake their heads, both tightening his hand on his gun.

"I.D., Ma'am."

"Oops! She forgot her ID at home, but I have mine."

Nate hands over a rectangular titanium key that

shows he's a VIP by its metal, thickness, and sheen even in the moonlight.

"Dr. St. Thiel?," the cop says.

His eyes color over to caution and even a hint of fear as he hands it back to Nate.

"Sorry to bother you, Sir. Just wanted to make sure you were okay."

"Fine, just fine, and as soon as we get some tiramisu we'll be better."

The cop looks at his partner, who makes a twirling rotation with his hand and she wonders if it's battle language to kill them both.

"Sir, I apologize, but we still need your fiancé's ID. A chink sub was spotted off the coast, and we're looking for Zeks. The federales are too. They'll bust our asses if we don't tick off all the boxes."

"Does she look like a Zek?"

Nate takes the opportunity to give her a big sloppy kiss on her cheek.

"Honey, are you some kind of killer sex cyborg?"

"*No* sweetie. You wish!"

They all chuckle a guy chuckle, and Lilith can feel Nate tense as if he's going to pounce on the cop.

Lilith has no ID, fingerprints, or retinal scan, and even

though they won't know exactly what she is they can easily guess even before they start tearing her apart to find out.

"Still need ID," the porcine one says. "Tell you what, ma'am, why don't you step out of the speeder?"

"Officers, this is getting silly. Perhaps I could just pay a fine tonight, you know, in silver or even gold, and you could forward it to the proper department tomorrow or whenever you get the opportunity."

The porcine one shakes his head.

The squirrely one makes a gesture, as if he's holding something between thumb and pointer fingers that he's sucking on —that Lilith interprets as sexual—and that could be good or bad depending on what he has in mind.

Very likely bad for him.

The porcine one shakes his head "no" even harder.

"Sir, is it true?" the squirrely cop says, ignoring the other's look of warning. "The rumor about Amirkhan/Bio_Wep?"

Nate stifles a smile and Lilith knows that means he has an opening her will ruthlessly exploit.

"Depends on which rumor exactly…?" says Nate.

"About Dragon Fly Hash," the squirrely one says, sticking his head into the speeder.

"D.F.H.?" Nate says, and reaches for the glove box with his good hand.

Both cops tense up, as he slowly pulls out one of two oily bricks of hash with a banded stamp of two 19th century Tong assassins over a dragonfly.

Nate hands the brick to the squirrely one who stares at it like it's sacred.

"That's an affirmative, officer. We developed D.F.H. during the Civil Wars to help pilots take the edge off their G-force accelerations while improving their visual acuity. Just doing our patriotic duty to win the war."

Nate salutes with his good hand and the man salutes back and his partner views them both with scorn.

"Fuck yes," the squirrelly one says. "Launched during the Scourging of San Diego!"

"That's right! Turned the tide. Also, between friends, it fuels the libido like jet fuel; lets you go all night even with multiple partners. Works like a charm, though not exactly legal; kind of a grey area. If you know what I mean?"

"Understood, Sir. We will need to confiscate this as contraband, but you can fill out a retrieval form down at H.Q. and ask for it back. Right? I think we can give your fiancé a pass on the I.D. for now. Chinks wouldn't create such a beauty."

"Thank you, officers. You hold onto that, and I'll be in tomorrow morning or at some point in the indefinite future to fill out those forms."

He seems to be winking at them, but it's dark, and

maybe his phantom limb pain is kicking in.

Either way, they take the brick, hand his ID back, and wave them on, with pig cop whispering in the other's ear.

"You stay safe out there!" Nate says and salutes again.

They both ignore him digging into the brick for a taste.

Nate rolls the window up and says, "G.E.D fuckheads."

Lilith sits, willing herself to stop shaking.

Are Amirkhans really this fucked up?

Maybe they did deserve to perish in the Kali Yuga?

They drive for a long time, both lost in their own thoughts.

"We were a pretty good team back there," Nate says.

"True," Lilith says. "Da Chi."

"Life from Death," Nate says. "So you play Go?"

"I dabble," Lilith says.

"I'm a first-level Dan black belt," he says.

He pulls out the other brick and expertly wraps a joint with one hand, takes a hit, and hands it to her.

She takes a puff and relaxes, driving just with her feet and knees, while bonfires on the beach reflect the drone's eyes with every light bracketed now by vivid columns that seem to bend to her.

Lilith has the feeling they are flying above the city, dropping precipitously before soaring up for the sheer joy of it.

Nate blows smoke rings as he holds his fingers contemplatively, even smiling at them.

"I might be willing to forget you maimed me if I can get to an ER? You can keep the speeder and all the silver you took from me. We amicably go our separate ways?"

So, it's Seki, or Dual Life where neither side can attack without losing and they must seek Dame, a move that ensures both parties' survival but doesn't move the game forward.

She sees no other choice that doesn't end with one or both of them dead.

"I can agree to drop you far enough away to give me time to drive off," she says.

Lilith can ditch the speeder and modify her appearance.

Maybe she can still make the sub rendezvous; beg the HIVE for another chance to serve and thus to live.

"Agreed," he says.

He offers the pinky finger of his good hand and she pinky shakes.

That's the best Lilith can hope for when the red and blue lights appear behind them again and then another pair with every flash sequenced now and subtle as a fugue.

"They want the other brick," Nate says, ever so slowly. "It's their retirement fund."

Nate uses his good hand to throw the hash out the window, and they must think it's a bomb because they swerve and one speeder crashes into a palm tree that bends but doesn't break as the car explodes and is engulfed in flames.

Lilith accelerates as shots ring through the speeder, looking like stained glass trailing tears, and she manages to dodge one by scrunching into a ball until her thumb is ripped off.

Nate is pierced through the middle and the speeder grinds to a halt next to a railing with the L.A. River fifteen meters below.

He is bleeding out with his W.Q. almost solid bone.

Despite her pain, she pushes his hair out of his face, and forces him to look at her.

She drops her voice two octaves and adds in overtones of his father who died when he was six and was known as such a strict disciplinarian that he would break rulers over Nate's knuckles when he misbehaved.

"Nate! Rally to me! You're dying, but I can save you."

"Out of R.N.A. pills."

"I have something stronger: direct transmission of

stem cells through symbiosis."

"Impossible," Nate says, "works in the lab and fails in the field. Both people die."

"There's an unorthodox way," says Lilith.

She points between her legs.

"No fucking way. I'm not losing my cock in that power saw pussy. I would rather die."

"You're confused again, Nate. My pussy is fine. And the world needs a brilliant scientist like you in such a dark time."

"You're right about that last part, but promise not to make me a eunuch."

"I promise sweetie."

She hands him the joint as she straddles him, avoiding hitting her lost thumb's raw aching wound.

When he says, between tokes, "Wait, will this regrow my fingers?"

Lilith stares at him dumbfounded.

How could someone so scary-smart they can splice insect genes into plants be so stupid?

"It won't turn you into a lizard, you idiot."

She scooches her dress up and panties aside, slips his pants down, and reaches for him in the flickering darkness as his eyes roll back in his head, and his breathing slows to static with them both slick covered in each other's blood.

Nate's almost dead but still erect as she slides him into her and rides hard and fast until she climaxes, releasing a tidal pool of enzymes, amino acids, and raw stem cells with a frequency of 432 Hz.

He climaxes at least a dozen times, and Lilith considers saving some of his seed as he might still win a Nobel Prize if he survives, though she isn't a breeder zek so sterile.

She keeps it anyway, as the HIVE will want samples for analysis, and possible khetization.

He opens his eyes as if reborn, grabs her arms hard enough to leave marks, and pistons the two of them together roughly, knocking the wind out of her until they both climax again.

Exultant, Lilith reaches up behind his neck to feel his W.Q. almost healed, so she slips her knife from her heel and uses it to pry off just as Nate stabs her in the back where she would have a heart if it weren't diffused through her system.

"Die!" Nate screams. "You crazy Zek bitch!" He stabs her again and again, drawing blood that is as red as any human's, and hurts just as much.

Lilith elbows him in the face, breaking his nose with a pleasing crack, just as the second police speeder crashes into them, buckling their speeder, and stripping the passenger door with the two of them holding onto each other not to be ejected while still trying not to be stabbed.

The porcine officer's face is filled with rage as he advances on them bellowing.

He jumps on the trunk, and smashes the rear window with the mace, covering them in powdery fragments of glass.

Nate stomps the speeder into reverse, causing the cop to skitter backward, drop his mace, and stagger. Nate quickly executes another stutter-step in reverse, and the speeder's rear severs the porcine cop's legs at the thighs, while the squirrelly cop fires point-blank, hitting Lilith in the chest, and knocking the air from her lungs.

Lilith drops to the floor and uses her wounded hand to accelerate the speeder through the railing, twisting in the air, the bullets arcing like lightning, and they land with a crash in the L.A. River's concrete bottom.

She is thrown from the speeder into a shallow stream of water, and Nate is gone; must have been thrown to his death.

She checks her la Pulse at the top of her head, preparing to leave through the crown.

She's covered with Nate's blood and her own, with the fetid water turning ochre under the street lamps. The Squirrelly cop spots her and fires, sending shards of concrete into her face.

Suddenly, water flows around her, lifting her up and downstream with the bullets whizzing by as she considers the green full Luna in the sky.

Even if the water takes her to the ocean, she will slowly drown as she loses consciousness.

Lilith traces the sacred symbol for peace, *Salam*, on her crown and chants Rumi Axiom #399: "Nothing ever truly goes away. The sun and the moon set, but they're not gone," as she sinks into the stream and her vestigial gills tear through her cheeks.

Lilith's saltwater tears merge with the freshwater as she assigns her Po-Soul to the depths before the darkness takes her.

MAGIC KINGDOM

Lilith wakes in a tank of water with pop garish illustrations of killer whales on the sides, filled with iridescent jellyfish, and two manta rays that swim around in equidistant circles.

She undulates, stretching her limbs, to see her left hand is webbed again with her thumb a black stub. Her bullet and stab wounds are filled with what appears to be pitch that burned her so badly it knitted her ribs on the left side together, so she is drifting in circles, same as the mantas, only in the opposite direction.

Her toes are now webbed and help her glide through the water.

Her Po_Soul's location at her femoral artery tells her that three weeks have passed since her date with Nate.

There is no external source of light, but she emits a faint greenish glow that attracts the jellyfish and keeps the mantas on track.

Her ancestors ate single-celled animals and plants and let them breed inside them until they were needed as emergency rations and also hijacked their photosynthesis to provide energy.

That primal survival mechanism must have kicked in saving her life, but someone had to tend to her wounds, and if they wouldn't free her, then eventually the HIVE cyanide would be released and no amount of nursing or algae would save her.

Also, what happened to Nate's W.Q. and Nate himself?

If he was dead, then she was dead too; the HIVE would tie her off as a loose end if the Amirkhans didn't dissect her first.

Why did Nate have to be such an asshole?

Jesus. Shiva. Kali.

Breathe, baby girl.

What are the Ajas?

The tank is topped by a series of bars with air above, but she cannot reach through.

She swims down to the bottom, made of stainless steel covered in script that she can read by her own light:

SeaLand was created in 1959 when Dennis "Skip" Johnson, VP of Marketing for Midwest Fun Corp took out an interstate map, pencil, and protractor and drew an arc between New York City, Pittsburgh, Detroit,

Chicago, and Cleveland, calculating that over thirty million blue-collar workers with over ten billion dollars of disposable income lived within three hours driving distance of beautiful Akron, Ohio.

SeaLand and all its affiliates were sold to Dizzy Corp in a liquidation in 1972.

Some ancient gulag?

No escape there, so she rises in a spiral, surveying the walls for a breach and finds more script near the top:

Attention Park Guests: If trapped inside the Pirates Town on Outcast Island, then we offer you a sincere Mikey, Molly, and even Spoofy apology!

Screaming will only allow water to fill your lungs.

So stay calm, keep your lips sealed, and flick the safety switch to your right.

N.B., Taking such action shows you waive all liability for Dizzy Corp and its affiliates.

The surface to the right is blank.

Further right is more script:

Sorry, stage right! A little Dizzy humor.

Then a sinister sigil: a black circle with two smaller circles on top and adjacent at forty-five-degree angles.

Lilith has seen that before but can't place where, and besides, she is slowly dying, and must escape.

She uses all her strength to push the red circuit breaker down and then back up.

Nothing happens.

She pushes down again, tearing her thumb open trailing blood, and pushes back up, and still nothing.

Then a maddening din of machinery makes the surface shiver, and the jellyfish dart left and right, ejecting black ink while the mantas keep their rhythm.

She remembers her purse and dives to the bottom to retrieve it as the concentric steel circle slowly opens, sucking water inside and then the jellyfish and the mantas too when Lilith realizes she will die if she doesn't move now.

She rises like a missile through the surface and grabs the bars but is unable to cry out with her gills exposed to air.

She can feel the water sucking her down from her neck to her thighs, feet, and then heels. The water evacuates in a whoosh, and she is left hanging by her webbed fingers when the grid slowly opens.

She crawls out to fall into a sluice that brings her up onto an aqueduct powered by solar cells. It slowly tilts her head down, but face up where she is unceremoniously dropped so quickly down a water slide she hydroplanes before landing with a splash.

She loses all sense of direction as she is bashed against

the pool's sides and into corpses and carcasses with dark figures swimming toward her when four strong hands reach down to pull her up and place her on the ground.

Her dress is torn so badly it barely hangs onto her thighs, exposing her skin to the atmosphere. She still has her necklace, so they are not common thieves. She trembles with the cold and fear too.

She is without a mission or files or training for any of this, so she feels helpless in a way she never did even with Nate.

Two human females stare down at her as she gasps for breath, her gills rasping, and her mouth and nose useless with her soft palate closed, and her tongue lying flaccid.

The first is blond and willowy, wearing Birkenstocks, jeans, and a Joy Division T-shirt.

She has a pre-Reckoning surfer smile but with the poise of royalty in exile.

The second one is voluptuous and wears an orange jumpsuit that says: **Los Angeles County Jail Inmate** on the back, black Converse sneakers, and a double strand of black pearls around her neck.

Her haunting beauty reminds Lilith of a Khmer queen: strong, square teeth like ivory; eyes cocoa brown; the corners of her mouth, eyes, and eyebrows, and the wings of her nostrils all slightly tilt up.

Her movements seem to ripple through her limbs,

and her dark brown hair is tied with a red bandanna that matches her cherry lips outlined with just a hint of azure.

Her skin tone is coffee with the palms of her hands peach.

Lilith has never known true desire before, and with Nate, the sex was like brushing her teeth: something she had to do, but she yearns for this woman in a way that she knows is irrational and doomed.

If the world burns, then she wants to be aflame with her till the bitter end.

"Eve, my pumpkin?" the first one says.

"Yes, Clare, my peach?" Eve replies.

"She's alive," Clare says.

Lilith is choking to death and they seem in no hurry.

"She flushed the tank?" Eve says incredulously. "I didn't even know that was possible."

"There go our plans for a carp farm."

"We should bring her in before it gets dark and let the big boss lady decide what to do with her," Clare says.

Lilith shakes her head no, but they ignore her.

Tactical training taught her never to allow herself to be taken captive, and Big Boss Lady sounds bad.

Very bad.

The sun sinks in the sky casting rose light against a park of fantastic architecture overlaid with baroque jungle; moss and lichen over every surface, pools of water full of orange turtles held by a single gargantuan leaf shaking as they swim, and palm and banyan trees twice the size of the buildings with the faint smell of the salt of the distant ocean mixed with an artificial scent like cordite.

Candy-colored buildings filled with statues and pictures of Zeks are everywhere and some of them still move robotically and even bark words through loudspeakers.

"Fine by me," Eve says. "I only work here."

They both laugh gleefully and place Lilith on a cart that says "Corn Dogs" with her heels hanging out the back and push her forward on an elevated track that is thick with vines, creepers, and hairy spiders the size of the women's hands.

Lilith shares the cart with a wide variety of scavenged greens and one tightly tied pigeon.

She is dying and needs a plan, any plan, to get away.

Perhaps she can slide off the side and dive into the water to escape. She tries to release internal valium, but she's empty after not eating for weeks. She slows her la Pulse to a glimmer of one beat per minute so she can survive until she has a chance to escape.

Her lack of blood and oxygen makes her dizzy and the women seem surreally elegant as they stride along above her.

"Two tapirs in the Rivers of Amirkha," Eve says.

"They're herbivores," Clare says. "No threat."

"Not necessarily, my peach. A mother with her pup so you get between them and you're trampled to death by mad momma."

"That's what happened to Madeline. At the Indiana Jones Temple and giant otters instead of tapirs, but same concept."

"Please," Eve says, "giant otters didn't take Madeline out! That girl was always getting herself and her kitty involved with people she had no business with."

"Like Dorcas, she got between those two equestrians and they murdered-suicided-murdered her."

"I prefer when they just murder each other and leave me and my kitty alone."

"Amen, sister," Clare says. "Oh! A jaguar at The Many Adventures of Winnie the Pooh!"

"That's not a jaguar, dear. That's a Sumatran Tiger. See the stripes and not spots?"

The tiger stands up, stalks to the water, and swims to the two tapirs.

The mother tries to herd her kid off, but the small one is frozen, bleating, and the tiger bites the mother's thigh with an audible crack and then descends on the pup, seizing its neck in a death grip.

A dozen crocodiles rise from the banks and swim toward the struggle in a strangely serene manner, their rear tails propelling them silently. They attack the tapir carcasses first and then overpower the tiger with their powerful mouths and tails lashing, ripping it to pieces.

"Run!" Eve yells.

They move to the front of the cart to pull it in a sprint while keeping an eye on the crocs.

Metal tracks extend up and away over the park as if defying gravity.

WINhuB had similar tracks, and Lilith had once ridden on them with her shamanic commissar when she was being taken to her public debut as a mermaid for park guests.

"Stay on the monorail and we're safe!" Clare yells.

"Leave the mermaid?"

"Keep her! I've heard rumors there was a Zek flash murder crew run amok that captured some Amirkhan/Bio-Wep VPs and tortured them to death. She might know something!"

"Wow. I like those Zeks already," Eve says.

They both laugh together the way sisters do.

"Right? Those Amirkhan Bio-Wep equestrians always pull that Do-You-Know-Wine? douche bag fuckery."

Lilith's eyes get wide and heart beat accelerates hearing Fatima's pet name for her.

Eve sees her respond and gifts her with a sweet smile and a wink.

"Adventureland or Frontierland?" Eve says.

"Frontierland is farther to base, but less water so will slow the crocs down."

Lilith's hand is dripping blood between the monorail tracks, and the crocs pick up the scent and trail them.

"Stop bleeding, baby girl," Eve whispers to Lilith.

She unwraps her bandanna and ties it around Lilith's hand.

"Komodos at three o'clock," Clare says.

"Hate those lizards," Eve mutters, "They smell like shit," glancing over her shoulder.

The Komodos cut them off by moving awkwardly onto the monorail.

"Main Street!" Eve yells.

They bump off the tracks with Lilith barely hanging on and move up a wide street with ransacked food courts on both sides and a multi-spired castle at the end.

They run past a statue of an ancient autarch holding hands with a rodent-bred Zek.

On either side of the street are dozens of X-shaped crucifixes with corpses nailed onto them, limbs akimbo, and signs written in blood hanging around their necks that say: Looter, Rapist, Cannibal.

The offending body part had been ripped out.

On their faces is the three-circled sigil Lilith saw in the tank, but now stamped in blood three times.

The Komodos get distracted by the rotting corpses, tearing off limbs and knocking the posts to the ground in a feeding frenzy.

An older one amputates a younger one's front legs when it gets too close.

"Right at Buzz Lightyear Astro Blasters!" Eve says.

They take a sharp right, and the Komodos gain so close that Lilith can smell their sulfuric breath.

"How are they running at dusk?" Clare says. "I thought they were cold-blooded?!"

"The mutations from the Solar Flares are still evolving all the animals!" Eve says as they run.

They bump off the tracks with Lilith barely hanging on and up a wide street with ransacked food courts on both sides and a multi-spired castle at the end. The gates are closed, and the walls are filled with holes from battering rams and scorched by burn marks caused by some great fire.

Lilith thinks she sees eyes following their progress from inside, but it might be a trick of the light from the torches that line the street.

They move past a statue of an ancient autarch holding

hands with a rodent-bred Zek.

On either side of the street are dozens of X-shaped crucifixes with corpses nailed onto them, limbs akimbo, and signs written in blood hanging around their necks that say: Looter, Rapist, Cannibal.

The offending body part had been ripped out.

On their faces is the three-circled sigil Lilith saw in the tank, but now stamped in blood three times.

The Komodos get distracted by the rotting corpses, tearing off limbs and knocking the posts to the ground in a feeding frenzy. An older one amputates a younger one's front legs when it gets too close.

"Right at Buzz Lightyear Astro Blasters!" Eve says.

They take a sharp right, and the Komodos gain so close that Lilith can smell their sulfuric breath.

They take another right onto the walkway for the Galactic Grill, with the crocs emerging under the water.

Clare says, "Take the Railway!"

They rise enough to get a view of the entire park, and the crocs and Komodos turn on each other, snipping off limbs and even faces as the women approach a domed complex.

A dozen or so orangutans sit grooming each other and munching on leaves.

Eve makes a hand signal to the leader: a gray old grandmother with a cowlicked female baby on her lap, who signals back, and then they pass unmolested.

Eve throws the pigeon behind them, and one nasty-looking Komodo swallows it, stopping only to lift its head and gulp it down.

The reptiles see the orangutans ranged around, and the grandmother pulls out a flute and makes a piercing whistling sound that stops them.

Still, one massive brute slips and slides after them when the doors open, and a woman appears with a flamethrower that says: **Property of Los Angeles Fire Department**.

She waves them in as she ignites the Komodo with a stream of superheated gasoline.

The lizard's body seems to melt from its bones, and the others register somewhere in their dull minds that this is a bad place for them and saunter away.

Clare and Eve lay panting as the woman coldly surveys them and Lilith.

She is rangy in a leather skirt fringed with tassels, a matching crop top, a turquoise necklace with a shell in the center over reddish-brown skin.

She puts down the flamethrower, making sure not to touch its nozzle, which is still glowing red, takes off her work gloves, and leans back and lights a cigarette against the super-heated steal.

She hands Clare and Eve each one, and they light from one another, blowing on the ends till they burn red.

They are in an open space like a cathedral with rising levels of concrete walls and metal spirals, with the dying light coming through cross-boarded and Plexi-glassed windows. There are a few stuttering torches and one solar Eddie Bauer lamp.

The floors and ceilings are full of cats that regard them skeptically.

Lilith crawls down from the cart and lies on her side clutching her purse and trembling in a fetal position.

"I told you two reprobates not to bring home any more strays!"

"She's dying, Sarah," Clare says, matching her glare.

"I don't give a shit! We're starving with nowhere else to go and don't want to draw any more attention than you maniacs manage just going out to get a pigeon and some greens. Now we're at war with not one, but two species of giant lizards!"

"They started it," Eve says.

She snickers, and Clare giggles.

"And technically crocodiles aren't lizards," Clare adds tartly.

Sarah shakes her head and uses her foot to push Lilith onto her back with an audible smack.

"You owe us a pigeon, bitch," she says.

Lilith is blue with lack of oxygen and can only nod, hoping to appease her.

"That necklace will pay the bill," Sarah says.

Lilith shakes her head, and so do Eve and Clare.

It's her only connection to Fatima, and she would rather die than give it up.

"Leave her be," Eve says.

"She can repay us later," Clare says.

Sarah crosses her arms and says: "How and when?"

But they ignore her.

"Breathe, baby girl," Eve says.

Lilith's eyes get wide, and they smile that she's responding.

"Who are you?" Clare says to Lilith and brushes her matted hair out of her eyes.

"What exactly are you?" Eve says.

Sarah squats down next to Lilith and surveys her face focused on her steel blue eyes.

"She, it—whatever the fuck—must have both criminals and cops after her because she has multiple knife wounds in the back and also a 9mm caliber exit wound too, and her thumb is nearly shorn off, so they definitely wanted her dead, and yet, she's still living; some uncanny tech right there. I say: we turn her over to whichever side pays the most for her soggy ass."

Lilith shakes her head no, but even that feels like a

heroic task, and her mind searches through all the possible Ajas and finds none.

She is completely in their power until she can breathe.

"And how do we do that without the cops or criminal harvesting us too, Pocahontas?" Clare says.

"Fuck you, bitch; you know my name is Sarah."

"With an H?" Eve says.

Winks at Clare.

"Yes, with an H, you can't abbreviate Hebrew, you Philistine. And if we don't turn her in, then tell me how we're going to survive?"

"We've always managed," Clare says.

"Managed? I haven't eaten for three days, and that was ten-year-old Twinkies scavenged from the Hungry Bear Restaurant."

"Their shelf life is a thousand years," Eve says. "So, there's plenty more where that came from."

"Fuck you, whore," Sarah says to Eve.

"What do you have against whores?" Eve says, nonplussed.

Sarah stands and puts her hands on her hips

"You know what? We have a show tonight for those equestrians that could make us flush, and you're inviting in a whole world of bad juju with this fugitive."

"Eve and I were fugitives when you took us in, Sarah," Clare says. "You didn't throw us to the wolves."

"Maybe I should have, Clare," she says. "Life would be a lot simpler."

"Lonelier too," Eve says.

Not joking this time.

The way Sarah looks at Eve, as if she cannot look away, Lilith knows she's in love with her, and Lilith can feel the tidal wave of her charisma too.

Eve checks to make sure her necklace is still there, fingering one pearl absent-mindedly.

Sarah looks away and then says, "Maybe. Anyways, get her put together and then out of here even if you have to dump her in the Finding Nemo Submarine Voyage."

She shakes her head and walks off.

Eve salutes and says, "Sure thing, Colonel."

Colonel?

Lilith needs to get out of there right now, as an Amirkhan colonel will identify her as a new gen HIVE Zek and execute her stat; except she still can't even sit up.

And she hates to admit it even to herself, but wants to stay with Eve.

Clare cradles Lilith's head in her lap and drops her forehead to hers.

Lilith allows herself to relax into her thighs and enjoy their strength and warmth and the thrilling feeling of her skin and breath washing over her.

"How can we help you, dear?" Claire asks.

Lilith sputters, her lips moving but only making a high-pitched keening sound.

"Blink if you understand," Claire says.

So many people survived and even thrived during the Reckoning by honing their capacity for cruelty, and this woman survived by being kind.

Lilith blinks twice.

"Eve, you were a medic during the Civil Wars. Do something!"

"Technically a vet tech pressed into service, but yeah, I have some tricks up my sleeve, though most people die regardless of what you do."

Eve leans over and gently opens Lilith's mouth and probes inside before taking a closer look at her gills.

"She's asphyxiating. I think we need to close her gills or whatever those things are, though that might kill her too. She's a piece of work, and I'm intrigued now. At the very least, we can trade her for a bounty."

"Always the opportunist, Eve," Clare says.

"It's a cold, cruel Kali world, my dear. Still have your sewing kit? Get the silver needles and silk threads, and I still have some myrrh that Tomas gave me."

"Tomas? That arms trader would sell his mother for a piece of gold."

"I don't have much need for mothers, but gold and myrrh have their uses, and so does Tomas."

Clare brings a pink Chanel bag, opens it, and hands Eve a silver needle and purple silk thread.

Eve then expertly sutures Lilith's gills, bringing tears to her eyes that Clare kisses away.

Eve covers the sutures with myrrh, propolis, and beeswax and then tilts Lilith's head back, causing her to gasp as her soft palate opens.

Still, she can't breathe.

Eve leans over and kisses her so hard her lips press open and her tongue pushes in until it feels like Lilith will swallow it.

Then she feels an unwinding deep into her lungs as they fill with life, pulling air from Eve's lungs.

She sits up and vomits water, snot, and blood, with Clare holding her hair out of the way and Eve checking her pulse and pupils.

Lilith tries to be strong and keep it all in, but they encourage her to purge, making cooing noises and lightly massaging her hands and feet.

More convulsions wrack her body as Lilith brings up

the now flattened bullet still covered in blood and mucus into her outstretched hand.

She drops it to the floor with a *thunk*.

"She's a Zek," Eve says.

"Impossible. They were all exterminated."

"They say the government and cartels keep some for research and playthings."

They exchange a glance, and Lilith can't discern its exact meaning, though she feels the sadness and fear in that look because she shared it herself with the Others, before they were Repurposed.

She must practice Sabaki; make subtle inroads into their territory by using Angle Play, so indirect and quick too, if she wants to stay here and stay safe from not only the Komodos and crocs and sign-language-using or perhaps even psychic orangutans and God knows what else was out there in the park, but the police and federales as well as A.B.W.'s security forces who have a reputation for playing rough.

Also, she can still barely sit up, let alone stand or escape.

"I'm not a Zek," Lilith says, her throat on fire.

She denies it the way her tactical training taught her too: spitting the word Zek out with an equal mix of contempt and fear.

It was easy, as many of the HIVE Zeks said "human" with the same derision as soon as they had vocal cords to do so.

She had heard that Amirkhans were motivated by sex, profit and malice, so concocted a story that included all three.

"It's a fetish modification my sugar daddy had done. It's purely cosmetic. I must have fallen into a coma after taking too many drugs at his fiftieth birthday party and fell into the pool, so they made a bet I couldn't survive and dumped me somewhere as a joke. The drugs slowed my heart enough that I survived underwater."

"He must be some sugar daddy — a patrician — to afford modifications like that," Eve says. "Sounds like a real asshole too."

"It doesn't matter," Clare says. "All that matters is you're alive. I'm Clare, and this is Eve, and the lady dressed as Pocahontas with the winning personality is Sarah. She's actually a total sweetheart once you get to know her."

"I'm Lilith. How did you find me?"

"Can I call you Lil?" Eve says. "You seem like a Lil."

Lilith nods, "Call me whatever you like."

She smiles at that.

Lilith smiles back.

She's saved her life twice now, and it's also an Approach Move: extends the Net to set up openings later.

"We were scavenging for mussels," Clare says, "out by Terminal Island when you washed up, face down at low tide, bleeding so much that you were attracting attention from Mako sharks in the water and proles on Long Beach."

"We put you in our cart and lugged you back to the park. We knew you needed water, and the tank by Splash Mountain is the only pool protected from the predators that migrated from the zoo after the Reckoning," Eve adds.

"Was there a man there too?"

"No man," Clare says.

Clare brings her a canteen and washes her face as she helps her sit up. Lilith feels her la Pulse wavering but then finds its rhythm. They lay her back on pillows with illustrations of the rodent Zek, and Lilith wonders why they aren't hiding the evidence of its existence, but the world is full of mysteries, and she needs to rest and recover if she wants to survive.

"It's showtime!" Eve says.

"Break a leg!" Clare says.

"I'll break two!" Eve says and disrobes, displaying an elaborate dragonfly tattoo with a woman's head on her back that wraps around her figure, with the wings spread over each scapula and the tail reaching down to her buttocks.

Clare has one too: a spider sitting in a web with very

human eyes.

They shower under the waterfall in the roof and then put on curious outfits as the sun sets through the open windows, casting a brilliant orange light over everything inside, the four of them included.

Clare wears a light blue ball gown with matching gloves that reach past her elbows, a black choker, and glass slippers.

Eve puts on a yellow skirt, blue blouse with red hearts on the sleeves and a stiff white collar, and gently unwraps the bandanna from Lilith's hand, wets the blood to her already red lips, and wraps it around her hair in a reverse tie.

She pulls out a pristine apple she had hidden God knows where and takes a big bite.

Lilith is exhausted, and her eyes close as she hears the sound of men arriving and rough laughter, Sarah's greeting, Clare and Eve with their voices several octaves higher now giggling.

The orangutans outside hit a wooden gong making a hypnotic atonal sound that lulls her to sleep as the cats climb to the roof and look down with their eyes glittering.

Lilith had never dreamed before; even the idea sounded like madness, but she dreams she is sitting with the orangutan grandmother who teaches her their odd but elegant language and how to care for the little ones, the plants in the jungle that nourish, others that heal, those that give visions from demons, and still others from angels, and one that antidotes all snake venoms though it only blooms when there is a full Luna, Mars, and Venus dancing together in the sky.

She tells the story of how the Grand Old Mother descended from the trees of the forest to venture onto the savanna in search of food for her children, where she struggled to stand upright to see the horizon, then the trees dying and leaving her all alone and stranded on two legs, and trying to find the path to the sea where all life began and will someday end.

She tells her of dreams of a future without fear of reptiles or mammals or man.

Finally, in the cold morning light, she pulls out a little flute, carved from bird bone, and teaches Lilith how to play to weave a prayer of protection around herself and her loved ones, and simply for the sheer joy of it.

KINDRED

Lilith wakes and is strong enough to stand, pee squatting against a wall, take a drink from the waterfall, and look around.

The central hall is lit by torches and floating lamps that slowly spin, casting beams of colored lights.

Dozens of men are dressed as princes and genies, jungle boys and elves, gods and heroes, and Zeks including the autarch's rodent-bred companion, and ducks and foxes too, monkeys and bears, dogs and rabbits.

A dozen women cavort with their princesses' costumes askew, some in armor, some lace, others with no clothes at all, but covered in brass, jade, and silver beads that shimmer in the light.

Many have terrible scars and wounds, missing digits, limbs, or eyes; others wear tiaras made of flowers, bone, or rose thorns.

They stand bent against a wall or on all fours, some

face up moving crab-like as they copulate, or intertwined with one another as the men queue on either side, talking so loud they are spitting, with their pants at their knees or ankles tripping, drinking spirits and smoking what Lilith now recognizes as D.F.H.

The Eleven Brothers each had eleven sons who often had similar orgies with the zeks at WINhuB, and though their costumes were different, the vibe was the same.

Men are men.

Eve stands like a vision of beauty between two equestrians: one dressed as a duck who stands behind her and the other as a dog in front of her.

She is still wearing the yellow skirt, but her blouse is gone, and her beautiful face lit as if with a fever, caught in her own rapture, oblivious of the men who fondle her buttocks, breasts, and sex.

The men argue, and the one dressed as a duck hits the one dressed as a dog hard across the face.

He responds by bashing the first's head against the wall until his mask falls off, and when he is struck again, Lilith can see his skull gleam by the firelight.

As he falls, he draws a derringer and fires into the dog's face.

The shot makes him stands perfectly upright for a moment, trying to pull his mask off before falling back lifeless.

Eve saunters away as if it never concerned her to begin with and is quickly surrounded by more men.

The equestrians pause for the briefest moment and look around nervously.

Sarah placates them by pairing them with new princesses and offering them shots of clear spirits and hookahs full of intoxicants.

Once everyone is distracted, she pulls the two dead bodies by their legs outside where the Komodos feast on them.

Lilith can emit pheromones capable of making a bull elephant climax— standard for all HIVE sex Zeks — but Eve must be emitting some military-level scent that's driving the men mad.

Something Lilith has never even heard of, though the HIVE keeps plenty of secrets from their Zeks.

She is concerned about how many times Eve can use the same Push-Through, or lethal attack, before she is the one pushed through.

Lilith also hates to admit it, but she's jealous of the men.

And even a little mad at Eve for encouraging them, though encouraging males' worst impulses is not only Lilith's job but her whole purpose for existing.

She stands and straightens her necklace, smooths her dress, and though her wounds still ache, they are healing enough to walk.

Her agoraphobia kicks in from the chaotic crowd, and she releases a strong dose of oxytocin, a trickle of Ativan for her nerves, and a significant amount of testosterone in case there's trouble.

She steps into a recess in the wall across from Eve and her veil of repulsive pheromones and overall rotting corpse demeanor clears a path through the crowd.

From there she can make out a man wearing a helmet like the ones the ancient mariners wore on Luna before they contaminated it with life and knocked it off its axis enraging the Urth's tides.

Except his helmet is round, resembling the rodent Zek sigil, with two other circles that look like ears but are likely transmitting devices. Instead of the visor reflecting the view, it projects the faces of the crowd—men and women—until it fixates on Eve's elegant image, mirroring it back to her.

So, a patrician using scramble tech to avoid identification, kidnapping, and assassination while slumming. A rare target in the wild and if she can engage him and secure his seed or W.Q. then that's worth ten equestrians. Since she's already free-range, perhaps she can negotiate handing over his assets to the HIVE in exchange for them providing the antidote to the cyanide and allowing her to go free.

He is already disrobed, revealing a sunken chest, a

paunch, and a small erect penis.

The two other men are tall and broadly built, wearing uniforms without insignia and wear swords on their hips — his bodyguards.

He punches Eve in her face with surprising force, knocking her slack, then picks her up and runs with her body tilting awkwardly in his arms in front of the dark recess Lilith occupies.

His guards jog behind him, looking left and right when Lilith stretches out her leg, tripping the patrician and nearly breaking her ankle in the process and being knocked to all fours.

Eve falls, hitting her head, and her pearl necklace splashes all over the floor.

Her face seems to melt, the bones softening, her eyes disappearing, and her mouth expanding to fill the empty space.

The patrician ignores Lilith, turns Eve on her back, spreads her legs, and enters her, not noticing in his frenzy the transformation reflected in his visor.

One of the guards kicks Lilith in the side and she doubles over in pain.

He pulls her hips up and her dress down while the other bodyguard unzips in front of her face.

Lilith tries to fight as the first guard digs his fingers into her sides, reopening her wound that bleed over him.

He recoils in disgust, and the other one slaps her face and pushes her head down to his erection as the first one enters her.

NudiBranches are able to hijack more than just photosynthesis from their prey.

They feed on Portuguese Man O' War and steal their nematocysts that they sequester in their skin like tiny grenades.

So, when he pushes her hand to his member 21,000 of them detonate blistering his sex and splitting it open like overripe fruit.

He staggers back to the wall, trying to salvage his virility in vain.

The man behind her is so engrossed that he doesn't even notice, his eyes closed and his breathing heavy.

Lilith invites him in as deep as possible until he lets out an audible sigh, his legs trembling as he climaxes right before she closes the first circle of 27,000 crystal teeth around his testicles and the second circle of 34,000 nano-fibered iron teeth around his penis stripping his manhood bare.

She makes sure not to release any Novocain, adrenaline, or dopamine to mask the pain.

He screams, shaking so hard he splatters blood all over Lilith before falling to his side and clutching his hollowed groin.

Lilith releases his reproductive organs in front of him, and he moans in horror at the sight of his ruined sex.

It only takes moments for him to pass into shock and die.

Eve slowly regains consciousness and instead of fighting, wraps her legs around her attacker's pale body.

She reaches for the back of his neck with one hand and passes her face through what isn't a visor at all, but a distortion field.

She kisses him so deeply he seems to wilt in her embrace before dropping her mouth to his neck, sinking her teeth in as if it were some permeable membrane.

He tries to get away, but she uses her legs and arms to pull him into her embrace even as his entire body shudders.

He climaxes and drapes over her lifelessly.

She pushes him off and sits cross-legged, staring at Lilith without eyes; her face, lips, and teeth smeared with blood.

The second guard backs up, covering his ruined sex with his hands, his ankles catching his pants and limiting him to baby steps. He pulls his pants up to his hips, shouts a blood oath, and draws his scimitar.

He catches Eve in the triceps of her right arm, shearing flesh, tendon, and bone.

Lilith tries to crawl over to put herself between Eve and the next blow but can barely move.

He raises his sword to behead Eve when Clare appears.

She drops the top of her ball gown, revealing perfect breasts, and then the bottom, showing a triangle of pubic hair between strong thighs.

She steps over the dead man in her glass slippers.

He turns to strike her, and she purses her lips to kiss but instead sprays viscous fluid, denaturing the flesh from his face, dropping the sword from his hand, and bringing him to his knees.

Sarah appears with a chef's knife and cuts the man's throat.

She also castrates the patrician for good measure and shoves his sex organs into his mouth for better measure.

Lilith pulls her clothes together and is suddenly filled with world-weary grief, curling up and crying.

Sarah moves the bodies outside where the Komodos feast on them.

Clare gently takes Eve's hand and guides her to sit against the wall.

The way she views Eve's altered features—with acceptance and even affection—shows that she has rescued her from her own worst impulses before and still loves her dearly, despite, or perhaps even because of her self-destructiveness.

Lilith wishes more than anything in the world that she had someone to accept her unconditionally, even if they knew she was a sex slave and a sea slug beneath the pretty face, figure, and lies.

Lilith can no longer keep her eyes open, though someone she knows is Clare from her gentle touch runs her hands over her wounds and lays her down on a pillow.

Clare or Eve or maybe both kiss her, and whether it's the shock or something they gave her, she falls directly into a dreamless sleep.

When Lilith wakes, the sky peeking through the roof is blue, the men, women, and corpses are gone, and Eve sits in front of Lilith in her county jumpsuit and black Converse, her face and body unmarred.

The cats surround her, snuggling their cheeks against her limbs.

The only clue of what happened the night before is her missing pearls.

"Hello, sleeping beauty," Eve says, giving her a light kiss on her still-healing cheeks.

The kiss feels so much more intimate than her rutting with Nate—who never even bothered to kiss her while she was saving his life — and inspires in her a desire to kiss Eve back, to open her lips and arms and legs — even her diffused heart—and please her every want, need, and desire.

But Eve isn't checking her out or admiring her face; there is something more in her gaze that communicates both longing and indifference, as if she already loves her but doesn't want anything from her. Lilith has never met anyone who didn't want something from her, or who didn't want everything, except Fatima.

Still, Lilith takes her hand in hers and brings it to where her heart would be if she were human.

"She's awake!" Clare says, back in her Birkenstocks, jeans, and Joy Division T-shirt.

She catches the moment between the two and, without the slightest jealousy, squats down and takes Lilith's hand to her own heart.

Lilith is overjoyed that Eve is alive and uninjured, but stumped how that's possible or what to say.

Her tactical training at WINhuB covered everything from how to use cutlery at dinner parties (outside in) to whether to have sex with a target's spouse, parents, or son or daughter to get close to them (yes), but beings—human or otherwise—rising from the dead was not covered.

The only explanation was that Eve and Clare were also Zeks—an Amirkhan cohort—which the HIVE thought was impossible without the North Korean technology, but she was learning the Amirkhans were mind-bending tricky.

They didn't seem to question how she overpowered

her attackers, so perhaps it was a don't ask and don't tell situation.

Still, this might be Hamete; a trick, and what seems the obvious answer could lead to disaster.

She had to be very, very careful.

Best to say nothing for now.

Sarah walks in wearing cut-off denim shorts and a crop top, and they all drop hands and turn to her, slightly embarrassed.

If she saw them or felt jealous, she hides it well.

"Look what we got!" Sarah says, and drops dozens of silver coins on the floor around Lilith.

Eve and Clare pretend to bathe in them, washing their armpits and their behinds, laughing.

Sarah adds, "And check this out: pre-Reckoning tech."

Lilith thinks she might pull out a ray gun, but it's some kind of toaster with a solar panel: a Belgium Waffle Maker and a bag of gluten-free family-size Belgium waffle mix.

"Waffles!" Eve cries in joy.

"I'll pour and you plate," Clare says.

"Fuck plates!" Eve says. "We have hands!"

They burn the first batch because they keep pressing the **Just a Little Bit More** button and finally get the settings right to where the flour still caramelizes without burning so it's more like candy.

Eve pours maple syrup over everything and then drinks directly from the bottle, licking the sap with her pink tongue.

"Eve," Sarah says. "You know that carbs make you bloated," trying to grab her waffle.

Eve pivots and escapes with a few ballerina steps, saying, "You just want more for yourself!" and takes a big bite.

Sarah sits down and watches her closely, lost in her thoughts.

"Waffle, Lil?" Eve asks.

"Still not hungry, but thanks." Lilith smiles at being asked.

At WINhuB, they literally fought tooth and nail over a teaspoon of algae.

"Lil," Clare says, "I forgot to tell you that we found your purse."

Sarah shakes her head. "According to salvage laws, that's all ours now," she says.

Lilith can see in her eyes that she knows that without Lilith risking her life, Eve would be lost to some patrician sex maniac's beachside estate dungeon or stuffed into an A.B.W. or other cartel lab to be dissected.

So, she softens and nods to Clare to hand it to her.

Lilith finds the bottle of Nate's RNA pills, opens it, and forces one down, feeling an immediate sense of well-being flood through her body and mind.

She offers Clare and Eve one, saying, "A little pick-me-up?"

Clare shakes her head, wrapped up in the waffle maker buttons while reading the instructions and eating.

Eve accepts, swallowing one and saying, "Va-Voom!"

She dances around the room doing pirouettes.

"Gift from your sugar daddy?"

"Yes, Nate, my sugar daddy. That fucker."

Lilith rustles through the purse, and there is no W.Q., but a D.F.H. joint wrapped in a hand-drawn picture of Lilith sitting by the ocean as a mermaid with a tail and outsized breasts, a red heart between her and a stick figure with an erection smiling and waving, and written under it: **Love You Lily! Nate.**

Did he hide it before or after the police first stopped them?

How could he have had time?

And why?

No way to know unless she had Nate in front of her to ask and she would be tempted to hurt him first.

She whispers: "Motherfucker."

"You okay, Lil?" Eve says.

"Sure, fine. Dragon Fly Hash, anyone?" Lilith says, holding up the joint.

"Yesssss," Clare says, laughing.

"So glad we saved you," Eve says, and kisses her sutured cheek.

Lilith hands Eve the joint, who uses a rodent butane lighter to ignite the blend and then sits back and takes a toke.

She blows smoke rings and holds her waffle sideways as Clare gnaws at its edges.

"D.F.H.?!" Sarah says. "Lil, you bought yourself another day's recovery! Now light me up!"

Lilith relaxes as they smoke, talk, and laugh, with the hash melting the boundaries, giving her a sense of floating in space.

Clare is not happy with Lilith's long matted hair held together by now rotten pink bows and offers a cut; a neat bob that frames her face.

Lilith lets her wash her hair under the waterfall, then brush it straight before cutting it with her tactical knife in a smooth wave. Clare reapplies her makeup a little heavier than Lilith likes, but it does add color to her cheeks. Eve kneads Lilith's back and then her feet gently, loosening her body to finally relax.

A calico cat sits in her lap, purring, and she runs her other hand over its soft fur as it arches into her palm.

With the D.F.H. infusion, she can see out through the holes in the patched windows with the now linear light tracking every granular detail.

She realizes with a shock that the odd mix of buildings is uncannily similar to the layout at WINhuB.

She remembers, as a child, being led through the WINhuB park by her shamanic commissar, confronted by crowds of people, especially children, who wanted to take photos with her, offer her all sorts of terrible fried food and neon candy, and gasp as she jumped into the pool, swimming submerged. They applauded before rushing down a flight of stairs to view her through tempered glass.

She carried a snorkel, mask, and fins to maintain the illusion that she was a human girl pretending to be a mermaid instead of a mermaid pretending to be a human girl. She was supposed to surface every couple of minutes to breathe and make a show of using them. But she had lost them on her dive and luckily no one seemed to notice as they gaped at her, and stuffed their faces with junk food.

Until a little girl in a pink princess dress and plastic tiara saw Lilith was breathing without the snorkel and started crying and then screaming as Lilith waved to her from the side of the tank.

Lilith could hear her shrieks even through the glass and couldn't take it anymore, so she surfaced and then ran back to her cell, where she was punished without food, sunlight, or communication for one month.

Even Fatima couldn't reach her.

Of course.

The HIVE and Amirkhan parks were all connected somehow.

They were the perfect places to manipulate humans to fetishize zeks as avatars of all their lost childhoods, innocence, and possibilities; pining nostalgically for a past that never existed, breeding contempt for the banal present, all the while ignoring a terrifying future slouching over the event horizon.

It worked except when the façade fell away and the humans' primal fears resurfaced to make them scream in fear.

When her solitary confinement was over, Lilith saw that little girl's mother in the WINhuB security block with a blank face like a doll's and swaying in a trance, so the parks weren't afraid to cull humans who discovered the secret.

She never found out what happened to the girl.

"What's wrong, Lil?" Eve asks. "Thinking about that guy?"

"No, just melancholy, I suppose. What is this place?"

"Space Castle in DizzyLand," Clare says. "You're not

from here?"

"No," Lilith says, startled by the question.

She has to be careful.

Guard against giving away too much information as well as the territory inside her heart.

She should have never risked her life for Eve last night, but she was happy she did and would do so again in a heartbeat. The HIVE didn't intend for her to stay in Amirkha past a single night, so they never gave her a cover story beyond kinky grad student.

"I'm from the Midwest."

"What part?" Eve says.

The weed makes her skin seem to glow; she's so lovely.

"Ohio," Lilith says. "Akron, Ohio. It's beautiful."

Both Clare and Eve laugh, scaring Lilith that she said the wrong thing and was found out.

"Akron is a shithole," Eve says. "But it's sweet that you miss your hometown."

"What did you do there, Lil?" Clare says.

"I worked at SeaLand," Lilith says. "Selling corndogs."

Eve and then Clare laugh so loud and hard the orangutans outside join in, and then Sarah too, and finally Lilith gives in and laughs so hard it hurts.

It does sound ridiculous, but does being a stoned sea slug bred sex Zek make any more sense?

Nothing makes sense, and yet Lilith has never felt more at home.

Eve opens the doors to a brilliant May day, and Clare joins her doing a conga dance while the orangutans point and laugh.

Some of the kids join in, though they can't really dance with their bowlegs, so they stutter step as Eve and Clare hold their hands.

The cowlicked one, beloved by the grandmother, reaches for the waffle, and Eve breaks off little pieces and feeds her, then just hands over the rest.

"Thank you," Sarah says to Lilith. "For stepping up last night."

"No problem," Lilith says, not sure what else to say.

Sarah, Clare, and Eve are a textbook San-San—3 Point Line, which are inherently unstable, and a fourth can solidify, but at the cost of breaking it into two pairs.

Lilith is still dependent on all three of them and can't see a way that unraveling can happen without destroying them all.

Sarah offers her hand, and Lilith shakes, enjoying the warmth.

That's when the screaming starts.

They step out onto the stairs to see the little one already dead in the grandmother's arms, eyes closed and mouth slackly open, and Clare and Eve writhing on the ground with bloody foam gushing from their mouths.

The grandmother holds the girl to her chest and keens to the heavens.

Sarah rushes to Eve, and Lilith to Clare, whose face is swollen and is clutching her stomach with her eyes glassy.

"Those motherfuckers poisoned the waffle mix," Sarah shouts to Lilith. "Keep her airway clear and let her vomit it out."

Lilith holds Clare as she trembles, bringing out cold clear bile.

They leave the grandmother to her grief and move the two inside, covering them with sparkly survival blankets as their skin is blue and cold to the touch.

Eve brings up blood and convulses as Lilith strokes her hair.

Sarah looks terrified and drapes her arm over both of them, helping them to purge, hugging them and telling them she loves them.

Outside, the grandmother cries out and strikes her chest with her hands, dancing erratically with the little ones looking on in horror.

It continues like that until nightfall, when Clare makes eye contact with Eve and mouths, "I love you, pumpkin," and closes her eyes for the final time.

Eve screams through the night, matching the grandmother's grief, and Lilith holds her in her arms as the animals in the park go dead quiet, listening to the two females mourn their beloved.

AFTERMATH

In the morning, Eve is deadly pale, with bloodshot eyes, and a swollen tongue but can sit up and drink a little water although she still brings up the bites of food she swallows.

No one says a word as Sarah washes Clare's body in myrrh oil, dresses it in a white linen shroud dyed with turmeric, marks it with sacred runes, and covers it in white Magnolia flowers.

Sarah kisses Clare's lips gently before closing her eyes.

Eve's cries reverberate through the air, so intense that snot streams from her nose. "I wish it was me rather than you," she wails, tearing at her clothes in anguish.

Lilith is at a loss for words.

Whenever one of the Others was Repurposed at WINhuB, she would weep silently in her cell, astonished by the salty taste of her tears.

She felt a deep shame, knowing the Others remained

dry-eyed, cautious of revealing any vulnerability that might mark them as the next target.

They put Clare on the cart, and when they pass the grandmother, she is lying on her back with her dead grandchild still on her chest.

Sarah gently dislodges the girl and covers her in a small shroud.

They put the tiny body in the cart next to Clare and trundle on to Main Street.

Lilith keeps an eye out for Komodos or crocs, but the entire park is eerily silent.

Eve follows them, stumbling and crying with her hair covering her face and oblivious to the world around her, lost in grief.

As Lilith walks down Main Street, pushing the cart with the two dead bodies, she feels an overwhelming sense of loss.

She never knew she could care about anyone living besides Fatima, let alone the dead, especially since she hadn't known Clare long.

How long does it take to feel connected to someone?

The Others at WINhuB didn't even have names (Fatima gifted her with Lilith when her designation was simply NhuB: 3243-293/11).

Just having a name made Lilith feel alive, human

even, rather than a piece of meat.

Then Lilith realizes that Fatima was likely Repurposed since she went missing.

So, she also has innocent blood on her hands.

Her heart sinks even lower and she staggers a bit and feels like just sitting down and crying.

But she has to go on for Eve and even Sarah, be strong for the people who saved her, took a chance on her, and who she is forced to lie to everyday for their own protection, but that doesn't mean she doesn't consider them family.

Lilith looks up, unable to mindlessly stare at the blanket covering the two bodies any longer, and takes in Main Street.

There's an Opera House that's silent as a tomb, the Train Station with all its trains still smoldering from a fire lit by lightning, the Cinema with an animatronics lady taking tickets and ghostly music from a piano somewhere inside.

The Fire Station has a single electric candle burning and for a split second Lilith thinks she sees a figure move quickly behind it, but when she looks again it's gone.

It's so strange; like a little town, but a town that no one had ever really lived in, and even the size of things is all wrong; with the second stories only 5/8 the size of the first.

Something that would trick human eyes into thinking the building is larger than it is, but Lilith's can see the ruse and many others clear as day.

The whole street runs to the castle which seems to stare back at them.

It all feels more like a masquerade, or a place for children to play make-believe, where adults give in to magical thinking.

Perhaps the surrealism made a half-mouse, half-man seem a plausible hero, or a dog-man walking a real dog appear commonplace. Or maybe even a sea slug hybrid could be someone you'd want to fuck.

Street lamps flickering cast eerie shadows that dance across the abandoned debris littering the ground.

There are artifacts everywhere—strange, colorful dolls and clothes filled with senseless eerie mantras, and empty strollers and wheelchairs—and the Zek statues and illustrations staring back at her seem to be grinning from the depths of their souls knowing the mad secret that brought everyday people her as if they were on a religious pilgrimage.

She wonders how many of them had felt the lash of a whip or sting of a cattle prod or true hunger that seems to hollow out your insides as she and the Others had at WINhuB?

She feels revulsion at the absurd mimicry but also a profound sense of loss, wondering what motivated the people who once walked these streets and the stories they left behind in this ghostly remnant of what must have once been a place of magic, hope, and dreams.

They reach the statues of the autarch and his rodent Zek and build a pyre using wood from the broken crucifixes.

Sara carefully places Clare's body in the middle, and Lilith carries the Orangutan child next to her, surprised by how light and fragile it is, almost like a doll.

Sarah takes out her tactical knife and strikes it against the concrete sidewalk, kindling a fire that quickly builds and gives off enough heat to singe their eyelashes.

Sarah chants, "We consign the worldly remains of our sisters to ashes and their Po_Souls to their true home: Eternity," then takes a torch and lights the pyre.

As the bodies go up in flames, Lilith recites Rumi Axion 669: "At the end of my life, with just one breath left, if you come, I'll sit up and sing."

Eve suddenly rushes toward the flames.

Sarah, bleary-eyed, restrains her, holding onto her as they both weep.

Lilith feels left out, but allows them their grief.

Eve looks up into the sky searching for something, only she knows what to alleviate her loss.

The flames illuminate her skin as if transforming her into

someone else. Lilith hardly recognizes her; she seems like a completely different person. The light in her eyes is no longer visible, her hair a tangled mess, and the emotions radiating from her are like a pain that Lilith can't fully understand, though she has also suffered terribly.

It is the kind of pain you should only feel if you are bleeding, or broken, or close to death.

They sit there all day as the fire burns out and there is nothing else to say.

As the sun begins to set, she notices movement in the castle and a pack of hyenas that dart back and forth across Main Street.

"We have to go," Lilith says. "Come on, Clare would have wanted us to survive."

She takes Sarah and Eve by the hand like children, up Main Street, and back past the Orangutans with all the grandkids holding the grandmother, and into Space Castle closing the doors.

They make a dinner of lamb's quarters and handfuls of tiny fish they scooped out of the Finding Nemo Submarine Voyage.

Everyone is silent until Sarah says, "The silver is bad too. Cut with brass."

"Why would they do that?" Lilith asks. "Just to be dicks?"

"No," Sarah says. "You know why. The patrician we killed, albeit in self-defense. It's revenge, and it's not over either. They could be on their way here right now to finish us off."

They all consider that with grim faces.

Even with the flamethrower, they would not last long against a squad of men with swords, maces, and guns. Or possibly a missile strike in the night as they lay sleeping.

Or just blast the doors open and let the Komodos and crocs do the rest.

"We kill them all," Eve says. "I don't give a fuck if I die either. I want them to choke on their own vomit like Clare did. We use the only thing they understand: Pussy and lots of it. We get all the princesses together and offer them a night they'll brag about to their friends, and then we get them inside and poison them or set them on fire or both."

"I don't know if that's a good idea," Lilith says. "They have Po_Souls, right? Or, I mean, they could develop them if given the chance?"

"People with Po_Souls don't poison innocents," Eve says, glaring at Lilith, who wilts in her stare. "Po_Soul-less cunts."

Sarah looks exhausted but shakes her head. "Lil, this doesn't concern you anymore. You did what you could and should be moving on at tomorrow's first light. You can't help us and will just be in the way."

"She's right, Lil," Eve says, gentler now. "Also, that guy friend must be concerned about you? You must want to get back to him or your family?"

Lilith has no family since Fatima disappeared.

She only has the HIVE, and they likely want her dead.

This is her home now and they're her family.

She wants what they have: the way they look at each other with such sympathy and connection and intimacy. She envies how Sarah gets Eve a cup of tea with a little bit of honey, not too much, without being asked, and how Eve leans into Sarah's shoulder, putting her head down onto her breasts.

Sarah wipes away Eve's tears with her own hair.

But Lilith has strict orders not to murder equestrians except in self-defense, let alone a whole batch of them, and maybe a patrician too.

That would mean the start of the Great War and her masters aren't ready for that quite yet. They still have people to kill, Khets to clone, nukes to hide within plain sight.

"I see. I mean, I do. I just…" mumbles Lilith

How do you tell someone you fell in love with them while another person who is also hopelessly in love with them is sitting there, and right after their beloved was brutally murdered?

Nothing in the tactical training covered any of the complexity of real life.

"I'll go," Lilith says. "That's best for everybody."

Eve stands and gives her a hug, and whispers, "A different place or time, and we might be together. But the die is cast, and to our separate destinies we go."

"Lil," Sarah says, breaking the scene. "You can clean up in a real washroom, and as far as I know, there is still water in the sinks."

Lilith realizes that's her cue to leave them to a war council.

Sarah is already plotting out white and black stones to represent the park and their angles of attack once the men arrive.

The black stones surround the park with all the white ones in the middle.

The bathroom is roofless and lit by sunlight, and the floor and walls are tiled in red, yellow, and blue with the Autarch's Zek peeking out of their corners.

"Fuck you, rodent," Lilith says under her breath as she pees, washes her raw but healthy wounds, and considers herself in the mirror.

Her dress is shredded and blood-stained with a bullet hole in the middle. Her necklace is on backward, and she rights it. She adjusts her face to make it more heart-shaped and blows out her cheeks so she doesn't look so craven.

She looks ten years older than her first date with Nate and realizes she doesn't even know how old she is to begin with.

The little girl freaking out at the park doesn't seem that long ago.

So many unknowns.

So few Ajas.

Lilith wishes she could talk to Fatima; even for a single minute, hear her gentle voice one last time.

She hopes against all logic that Fatima is still alive out there somewhere.

"What do I do?" Lilith asks her reflection in the mirror.

New Mandarin script scrolls across the mirror:

Target 2: Emon Luxk 9.0

Mission Objectives:

- **Retrieve WQ**
- **Discern Amirkhan/NAS_SPAC's Predilection Toward Further Space Exploration**
- **Release Target Alive & Unharmed**

She's surprised it's not a terse "Self-Terminate" message repeated three times.

So, they found her and accepted she was in deep cover.

Perhaps that was even their plan all along.

They must have retrieved Nate's W.Q.

She is even more surprised by the target: Emon Luxk.

Emon Luxk wasn't a patrician but *the* Patrician.

He privatized the Amirkhans' space program when the government finally admitted they couldn't accomplish anything significant on their own and sent a million Amirkhans to the planets, moons, and asteroids of the solar system until they all died from radiation during the Solar Flares.

If she can secure his W.Q. and seed, then the Great War was already won, and she might be able to parlay her mission into a pardon or even freedom.

She feels renewed with purpose and grateful to the HIVE for giving her a very rare second chance.

Then the Elven Brothers' chop appears across the mirror, except now it only has ten lines.

The top one is missing.

That's bad.

Very bad.

Father Brother is either dead or wishes he was dead.

Ten in the I Ching symbolizes: *Treading Carefully.*

So, the HIVE Brothers' struggle—each a king in their own right—for global supremacy begins setting all the other pieces in play: ruthless queens, savvy sloe-eyed concubines, shamanic bishops, psychopathic knights, and even pawns like Lilith who can only move one step at a time unless they—against all odds—make it across the board to become queens.

Targeting Luxk was a God Move: a single decisive play to win or lose everything.

She had no idea how she would target him, as he likely either lived in a fortified fortress or perhaps a radio-active-shielded bunker on Luna or Mars.

She would do her best.

Scanning his files internally, the only anomaly is he has nine sub-files: Luxk 1.0, Luxk 2.0, Luxk 3.0, etc.

Some are concurrent for a week, and others separated by three-month increments.

The last one (Luxk 9.0) was updated two days ago.

Possibly, the overlap could be explained by powerful stimulants some whispered his people brought back from other worlds that give demon-like focus but also caused schizoid breaks after the first week awake.

He's an Asperger genius with a messiah complex who still plans to colonize the solar system despite the Flares killing everyone already there and all the surviving rockets rusting on their launch pads, with no fuel, computers, or astronauts to replace them, and the solar ionizing radiation still so strong that you can see the aurora borealis in the middle of the day.

He's a Nestorian Christian, so he believes in the separation between God and man, and since that gap is so vast, he might as well try to bridge it.

If he can't bring the heavens to mankind, then he can bring mankind to the heavens.

So Lilith will give him a little taste of heaven too and

everyone gets what they wants: win-win.

Lilith feels sure of herself now that she has a mission and a reason to stay longer with Eve.

Eve and her can be a team together that no one can beat and though she can't replace Clare, she can love Eve just as fiercely.

Clare showed her the way, prepared the path, and now Lilith would complete it even if it consumed her.

She goes back to the war room.

It used to be just a room with peeling pink walls, but now it's their war room.

Those equestrians are so, so fucked and Luxk too.

Game on.

EVE

Lilith squats next to the two women and takes one black stone and drops it in the middle of all the whites at the Mad Tea Party.

"I'm not going anywhere. We all need each other to pull this off."

Eve gives a glimmer of a sad smile, and Sarah regards Lilith skeptically.

"We need to play a snap-back. Offer a pawn for sacrifice. Then spring the trap. We get them all in one place with their pants down and do a Monkey Jump to catch those fuckers in the crossfire."

Lilith drops black stones at the borders of the entire park.

"I'll be the pawn," Lilith says.

"I'm the pawn," Eve says.

"We can all be pawns," Sarah says. "Go on, Lil."

"We invite them to the Mad Hatter Tea Party, interrogate them in Alice in Splendourland, and then channel the guilty into Main Street."

Lilith drops a trickle of white stones from The Mad Hatter Tea Party Alice in Splendourland to Main Street ending in a pile right in front of the castle.

"They'll give in to instinct and run to escape, and that will be their undoing. Right into the killing zone. When we are done exacting justice, we use the Yellow Horseless Carriage to escape into the prolehoods."

Sarah looks at the stones, but Eve stares directly at Lilith with what she is a little ashamed to admit to herself is admiration.

Even Sarah seems impressed.

"We play under the stones; give up territory in the beginning to gain everything in the end. I need one thing, though: afterward, I need to find Emon Luxk and fuck him."

Sarah actually laughs and shakes her head.

"That's all? Perhaps we should invite the Senate Syndicate and you could fuck all of them too."

"Why?" Eve says.

"Why what?" Lilith says.

"Why do you need to fuck Emon Luxk?"

Lilith falters, knowing what a stupid thing it was to

say.

It was like Eve showing up at the HIVE and demanding to fuck the Big Brother, or whatever little brother was the Big Brother now.

Still, she has to say something.

Something perversely Amirkhan.

"My sugar daddy had a cuckold kink and wanted the biggest alpha male to have me before he would take me back."

Sarah and Eve stare at each other and then at Lilith with unalloyed skepticism.

"Luxk was the patrician we killed the other night," Sarah says. "At least we think he was since no one else has a scramble helmet that we know of."

How could that be?

The HIVE had telemetry on most the Amirkhan equestrians and some of the Patricians too.

Luxk had to be alive.

Even if he was on Luna, they would at least know his heart was still beating, if not his exact location.

But she saw him killed less than 48 hours ago.

Even with the uncertainty, the snap-back was still the best play.

Her only play, really.

Out of Ajas.

"I can't say anything else without putting you in jeopardy, but I can promise gold afterwards."

Eve glances at Sarah who searches her eyes for something; perhaps to see if she has taken Clare's place and now realizes she never will and might as well try to get them all a pay day and move on before their luck runs out.

"I'll talk to Tomas," Eve says. "Do a little fishing and see if Luxk really is alive. If so, then we tell him we have all the princess pussy in the world! All thirty-two of them! Tell his equestrian friends and Luxk too."

"No, Eve," Sarah says. "Telling Tomas is too dangerous. If Luxk's dead, then they'll figure out that you killed him and send a team to extract you. Remember Rabia? They cut her feet off after she only slapped a patrician, let alone murdering one."

"It's the only way," Eve says. "Listen, I know Luxk is the one who did this."

"How?" Sarah asks. "How can you know?"

"Because he got me pregnant the month before," Eve says. "And this was his way of ending the pregnancy. I miscarried last night. Twins."

She touches her hand to her belly and winces, and Lilith realizes how very dumb she is, and how much she misses seeing what is directly in front of her.

Sarah's eyes cloud over with darkness, but she doesn't

say anything.

She just lowers her head and rubs her temples.

"I am so sorry," Lilith says.

Eve shrugs but looks haunted.

"If Luxk is alive, then maybe I'm mistaken. Either way, we will find out."

Lilith is stunned.

If Eve is a sex Zek, she should be sterile like all the Others except breeders.

Killer Zeks often have sex with their targets too, but shoot blanks—their semen and not their bullets, which are live rounds.

Even with breeders, the HIVE almost always harvests semen from targets for khetization instead of allowing the pregnancy to proceed, as all the offspring born from the union of human and non-human so far have been stillborn.

Breeders really only exist to birth more Zeks a thousand at a time, after which they die from exhaustion.

Or perhaps Eve's a sterile sex Zek like Lilith and doesn't know it and her child was doomed from the start?

She can't ask Eve if she's a Zek without her and Sarah asking her, so again it's a don't ask and don't tell situation.

"It's for the best, Eve," Sarah says, but doesn't sound

convinced herself.

"Let's move on," Eve says.

Though Lilith can tell she hasn't moved on.

Not at all.

"It's settled then," Sarah says.

Picks a fish bone out of her teeth.

"We lay low for a month and then spring the trap. If we find out that Luxk is still alive, then Eve can determine if he poisoned her and Clare. If he didn't, we let Lilith fuck him, let him go, and know it's one of the equestrians who were here last time."

They hold each other's hands, keeping eye contact, knowing they are likely going to their own deaths. They finish eating and go to separate corners to sleep a little as the grandmother orangutang mourns outside.

Later, Eve comes over to Lilith and snuggles into her embrace, and Lilith holds her as she cries through the night.

***

The next three weeks, Lilith and Eve sleep during the day and work at night to avoid watchful eyes; so they have to be wary of nocturnal predators, though most are scared of Sarah's flamethrower, which she lights periodically to let them know they are not easy prey.

At the light of dawn, they snuggle together under a

sleeping bag covered in illustrations of the rodent Zek and his lover, and if Sara notices or cares she gives no indication.

They salvage wooden ties and iron spikes from the Railroad that Sarah uses to sequester the southeast section of Fantasyland forming an isosceles triangle from the Matterhorn Bobsleds to Mr. Toad's Wild Ride to Peter Pan's Flight with the only escape to Main Street.

Lilith sometimes wakes in the middle of the day and watches Eve sleeping with her eyes under their lids moving in dream time, her breath soft and supple, and her limbs trembling from the fatigue of their work.

She kisses the top of her head, forehead, and lips, and Eve smiles, eyes still closed, and turns and snuggles into her warm as the cats.

***

One moonless night, they spot a dirigible, **Senate Syndicate** written on its side, and Eve pulls Lilith under the Corn Dog Cart until it passes noiselessly, seeming to swim through the atmosphere like a giant whale.

"That's bad news," Eve whispers. "I haven't seen an S.S. airship since the Civil Wars, when they used them to nuke dissident groups, cults, and outlaw enclaves."

They wait for it to pass before they move, and Eve tells Lilith to stay very close to her—not to stray or wander—as the park is not what it seems and there are parks within parks, and Lilith wouldn't want to be a guest in any one of them.

The way Eve says it, looking away, Lilith knows she speaks from personal experience.

***

One moonlit night, they spot a beehive tucked under the eaves of the monorail thirty feet off the ground.

Eve grabs hold of the trestles and with startling speed swings herself hand by hand up till fifteen feet where she turns, smiles, and winks.

Lilith stretches out to her limit and grabs ahold with the cold steel beneath her grip emitting a thrumming feeling as if the electricity were still on that makes her tingle head to toe.

They reach the hive and tuck themselves next to it with their toes pushing one side and their backs another they can stay aloft with the tension alone.

The hive is nearly silent with a dozen bees at the opening bearding the wax and flitting their wings.

There is the feeling of expectant sensuality with the smell of wax, honey, and propolis and also danger if the fifty thousand bees within were to wake and swarm out in fury, stinging them to death even before they hit the ground.

Lilith realizes with a start that this is the hive where Eve sourced the propolis she used to heal her wounds when they first met.

Eve makes a "silent" motion with her finger to lips and slips her lithe hand and then wrist right past the guard bees who seem not to notice and withdraws her hand glistening with honey, red propolis and semen-white royal jelly.

She offers it to Lilith who, heart beating like a drum, licks it off as Eve keeps eye contact, and the sweetness of the honey is overwhelming with the propolis medicinal sour, and the royal jelly so pungent it makes her gag a little.

Eve disrobes and covers herself with honey and Lilith feels like her most important mission is to not miss a single drop as they make love with the torque of their bodies twisting to keep at least a foot or hand on the rail and the other on each other, as they fall into each other as if into fathomless depths.

After, they swing down the monorail hands still sticky and find each other's fingers as they walk back to Space Castle.

Eve whisper in her ear.

"The only difference between a queen bee and a worker bee is how much royal jelly they eat."

She pinches Lilith's behind, causing her to let out a playful faux squeal.

"We will have to double your diet of royal jelly then my love," Lilith whispers back and kisses her with the taste of her own sex still fresh on Eve's lips.

"Yours too and straight from the hive," Eve whispers back and pushes her thighs into hers exaggerating a bow legged walk.

"Deal," Lilith says, and they shake pinkies, still wet with dew.

Lilith feels high with the rush and strangely enough when she puts her hand to her now beating heart it's not diffused at all, but dead center in her chest.

She feels strangely powerful with its slow steady beat matching Eve's.

Also incredibly vulnerable knowing that though her sex is still protected by rings of adamantine teeth and her mind by her million-to-one survival at WINhuB that now her source of strength is also her greatest weakness; so soft, organic, and alive it's like a hive with all the killer bees off hunting pollen leaving her true home unprotected and dripping with honey for anyone bold enough to take it.

For the first time, Lilith feels truly human.

***

The week before the party, an old couple, the woman white and man black—old even before the Reckoning—walk the grounds unmolested in matching rodent Zek jackets and four-fingered gloves, pointing out scenes from their very own memory lane, and smiling and holding hands the entire time.

Even the Komodos let them be.

As they watch them, the back of Eve's hand brushes Lilith's and she doesn't know what to do besides enjoy the feel of the warm skin on her's.

"Could you imagine," Eve asks, turning to her, "growing old with someone and being just fine in all this madness?"

No," Lilith says, "I can't."

Aware of how even while grieving, how vital Eve is; the way she stands on her tiptoes to see into Lilith's eyes, the musky scent of her skin, her eyes so bright they almost give off sparks.

"But I want to be able to imagine that kind of joy. I really do."

"Let me show you something, Lil."

"Sure."

They take a hidden passage into Frontier Land and pass the spot where Clare and Eve first rescued her from Splash Mountain. They stop in front of what Lilith initially mistakes for an altar: a massive stone with a triangular base rising into a jagged obelisk.

Someone has scattered rose petals at its base.

"It was the autarch's," Eve says. "Fifty million years ago, a flood covered a forest and the silica in the water froze this tree into sandstone."

"Humans saved it because of its beauty?" Lilith asks.

Eve brushes her hand and then takes her fingers, slick with sweat, into hers.

"No dear, there were no humans then. It was so long ago that the highest point on Earth was still underwater."

"Mount Meru? The axis of the world? Was under the waves?"

"Yes dear. Mt. Meru was underwater just like this tree."

"The time frame makes me feel so small. So insignificant."

Eve turns and caresses her cheek.

Lilith accepts her hand and turns into her fingers.

"I don't know about you, Lil. But I'm tired of feeling small. I don't ever want to feel small again. I want to be bigger than anyone who wants to hurt me again. People like them are always hurting people like us. Sometimes just for sport."

"I feel that pain too. Of being a slave. But I don't want to feel bigger than anyone, just to have my heart swell with someone special: with you. And I already have that feeling right now here with you."

A tear forms on Eve's cheek as she blushes, and Lilith kisses it off.

"Thank you, Lil. Let me share something else that will make us both feel big."

Eve leads her by the hand through switchbacks, and over banks of fallen trees, through walls, and around attractions.

Lilith struggles to keep up in her heels as they enter Fantasy Land and into the entrance of a glade hidden by the ruins of a jet liner that had crashed during the Flares.

The ground is littered with skeletons, and the soil is a rich loam that gives rise to a burst of soft grasses mixed with mint, thyme, and sage.

Around the edges, there are orchards in a riot of colors—boysenberries, honeysuckles, and dwarf cherry blossom trees.

Small ponds of water hold white, red, and purple lotuses dotting the surface.

"What is it?"

"It's a garden, baby girl."

"Like an oasis?"

"Yes, dear. A secret oasis of beauty amidst all the misery. Just like you."

Lilith is the one to blush this time.

She has never felt the sensation before; heart rate rising, a slippery, coppery taste in her mouth, cheeks burning with blood.

"Sweat talker," Lilith says coquettishly and dips her forehead to rest on Eve's shoulder.

"Sweet walker," Eve says, and it's so silly they both laugh.

Lilith leans on Eve's shoulder as she removes her high heels, making them the same height as they walk hand in hand onto the grass.

A single apple tree stands in full sunlight, its branches heavy with ripe, red apples.

The lush green leaves and swollen fruit create a vivid contrast against the bright blue sky.

In the background, the Matterhorn rises, its snow-capped peak piercing the heavens and providing a stunning backdrop to the serene scene.

The tree's gnarled trunk and sprawling roots suggest it has weathered many seasons, standing tall and steadfast amidst the ruins.

Eve leans gracefully against the tree with the clear daylight shining on her hair and brown skin as if caressing her.

"No one else knows about this," Eve says and brings Lilith to where heavy branches hang low with fruit.

"Maybe we should be careful," Lilith says. "Perhaps others know, and it's poisoned or a trap of some kind. You know, a *Net*, in Go."

"Don't be silly, baby girl. I've been eating them since day one. Where do you think I got the apple from when we first met? The Refreshment Corner Hosted by Coca-Cola?"

"I trust you," Lilith says.

Somehow both frozen in place and on fire.

She thinks Eve will pick one from the tree, but instead,

she gently pulls Lilith into her arms with an apple between their faces and kisses its surface, gesturing Lilith to do the same while maintaining eye contact.

The rind's texture is unreal, considering Lilith has mostly eaten algae, canned sardines, and once in a while, on special occasions, a Man O' War.

Something else too though, it tastes like freedom.

Love even.

Eve makes a "One, Two, Three" motion with her fingers, and they bite at the same time, tasting the flesh and then another bite and another until their lips connect around the sweet pulp and bitter core in such sync that they swallow the seeds together.

"I'm falling in love with you, Lil," Eve says, "I know I shouldn't so quickly after Clare, but I can't help it," holding her hands with fingers interlinked. "You're different than anyone I've ever met, and I can't get enough of you."

Lilith wants to say it back but didn't even know love was real until she met Clare and Eve with her entire existence about survival, and beatings, and then preparing for missions and the coming war to end all wars.

She manages, "Eve, my Jan," the Persian word for: My Soul.

Eve responds, " Lil, my Mer," that means: Beloved.

"One day," Eve whispers, "Together, hand in hand, we will enter the Oasis."

Lilith trembles in joy that her love is also on the Path to the Oasis and wants to ask so many questions.

But as she opens her mouth, Eve touches her lips to hers again with a sweet sigh of pleasure, and Lilith melts in her arms, barely kissing back but letting Eve hold her and run her lips and tongue against hers, savoring the sweetness of the fruit and flesh.

Their first committed kiss is over far too quickly, and they both look away as the sun rises over the castle.

"Here," Lilith says. "I want you to have these to replace the ones you lost."

She takes the strand of pearls off and clasps them to Eve's neck.

They are nearly exact replicas of Eve's lost pearls except they are white instead of black.

"They were given to me by the only other person I ever loved. Before I met you, I mean."

Eve slips into the pearls and kisses Lilith so hard it hurts.

They both feel eyes upon them now and sprint to the edge of the garden, Lilith leaning on Eve's shoulder as she fumbles to get her heels on, and they hustle back to Splash Mountain without mentioning it again, though the feeling of Eve's lips lingers on Lilith's like a promise.

While she sleeps, she dreams that she and Eve embrace in a temple built of black sandstone on top of an active volcano with two moons in the sky: one full and blood red and the other a dark crescent.

She wakes startled, and leans into Eve, who murmurs and kisses the tips of her fingers with a dozen cats snuggling at their feet.

AGAMEMNON

It rains, with big cumulus clouds blocking out the sun.

Lilith sits in a window on the second story drinking mint tea harvested from their garden, surrounded by cats she feeds catnip to, and considers the park stretched out in front of her.

It's become her home, and the pattern of some of the lights still coming on just after sunrise powered by solar and a couple of rides still firing up is reassuring that some good things survive even during times of darkness.

Her eyes always end up on the Matterhorn, hoping it would start even for a minute, but it never does.

The castle squats like a wounded goose and she instinctively leans back to stay out if it's line of sight.

"Is that you up there, my jaan?" Eve yells, cupping her hands around her mouth.

Lilith smiles down at her.

Eve climbs up and snuggles next to her, taking a sip of her tea and kissing her with the honey on her lips, and they make love with the cats around them purring and the raindrops splattering over them.

After, Eve asks, "Were you daydreaming, baby girl?"

"A little," replies Lilith, "and feeling content for the first time in my life."

Eve smiles and kisses her neck. "Maybe, after we get justice for Clare, we can spend some time together outside the park?"

Lilith can't believe her ears.

They had never talked about the future; they knew they would die in the coming battle, or the Great War, and even if they didn't, the Kali Yuga was coming on fast with the ocean in the distance closer every day and Luna further away in the sky and sometimes disappearing completely.

"Perhaps we will grow old together?" Lilith says, her face blushing and every cell in her body craving a "Yes," as she thinks of the ancient couple in the park holding hands.

"Let's see," Eve says, kisses her cheek, and climbs down.

"Okay?," Lilith says, but Eve is already gone.

She finishes her now cold tea alone and even the cats wander off.

∗∗∗

They all need a break, but Eve has a copy of the Penguin Edition of *The Greek Tragedies* and insists they perform the first play: *Agamemnon*, where the Greek warlord is killed by his wife for sacrificing their daughter to the goddess Artemis to win the Trojan war.

She waits until he is in the bath and throws a net over him while her lover brings an ax down.

Eve will direct, play Agamemnon, and the goddess Artemis.

Sarah will play the vengeful wife and her new lover and co-conspirator.

Lilith will play Agamemnon's new concubine, Cassandra, a prophetess doomed to foresee the future no one believes, and Agamemnon's murdered ghost.

They use DizzyLand princess costumes for the female characters' outfits, and Lilith, as the daughter's ghost will wear a mask with eyes wide in terror, mouth scrunched up in a rictus, and blood smeared over it.

She will be lowered into the scene by a rope offstage.

Agamemnon wears a rodent Zek head to signify his power, and Sarah scavenged a real ancient bronze Greek sword from a museum, and its edge is still so sharp they use it to cut vegetables when making soup.

Eve is constantly making notes in her dog-eared pages of the book, and both Sarah and Lilith want to ask her why this play and why now, but they both are in Eve's thrall and figure it's good therapy to help her grieve Clare's death now that their work is complete.

Except, Eve never mentions Clare, and she seems happier than she ever did, though she can be hot and then cold, like the time at the window.

But Lilith hopes she gets it out of her system, and after the play and massacre that they can move on with their lives.

It's a tricky production because it requires multiple costume changes, the actors to play not only against each other but themselves too, and everyone to be part of the Greek Chorus, with some of the orangutang kids filling in the ranks in exchange for banana popsicles Eve salvaged from The Main Street Fruit Cart, but they tend to wander off during the most dramatic scenes.

There is a tense moment when Lilith gets stuck halfway while being lowered onto the stage by Sarah and she slowly turns in a circle using her arms and legs to try to right herself.

She manages to maintain her composure and deliver her monologue before Sarah cuts her down, and she lands with a thud, scrambles to her feet and takes a bow to the audience of orangutangs who erupt with laughter and applause.

All three of them take bows and clap for each other, and in that moment, Lilith forgets all about the coming battle and Great War and Kali Yuga as she stands hand in hand with Sarah and Eve on the stage.

**

They never get to perform the next play, *The Libation-Bearers*, because Tomas shows up unannounced, but also right on time.

There's a knock at the door, and Sarah picks up her flamethrower, and Eve a bat, and Lilith the Eddie Bauer solar lamp, but more to be holding onto something than self-defense.

"Ladies?" a happy and cultured voice calls out, "The door is now locked? No?"

"Tomas," Sarah says, rolling her eyes but keeping the flamethrower ready.

"Tomas!" Eve says, dropping the bat and pushing the doors open.

Tomas is short, fat, and has curled platinum blond hair that falls to his chubby cheeks, making him look like a cherub.

He wears bifocal glasses secured with a faux pearl bead necklace and what appear to be black pajamas covered with red and green toucans and matching flip-flops.

He carefully removes his flip-flops and leaves them at the door.

His face has the preternatural glow of a tween boy, but when she looks closer, she sees he has the beginning of jowls, bags under his eyes, and enormous pores on his nose, all artfully camouflaged by concealer.

Lilith was expecting an alpha male, but he looks like he should be baking pastry.

"My dear," he says, spreading his short arms out as wide as they go.

Eve rushes into them and then takes a peek out the door and ushers him in, closing it behind her.

"Where have you been?" Tomas asks, looking genuinely concerned. "I had a new pair of accessories, and you never came, so they went to," and he looks at Sarah, who gives him a hard stare as Lilith wonders if he is distantly related to the rodent Zek.

Eve nods at him to go on and speak freely.

"*Waste.* I mean, I was going to recycle them, but they were bespoke for your perfect form."

"You're the arms dealer?" Lilith asks.

"Oh my god," Tomas says. "How crass."

"She's from Ohio," Eve says, not unkindly.

"Akron," Lilith says. "It's beautiful."

"Ooooo...that explains a lot. I was actually a tailor pre-Reckoning, and now I'm an arms dealer of sorts; though I'm proud to offer a full suite of services and even have been known to steal a heart or two."

He gives a big smile and Lilith can't help but smile

back at him.

Sarah frowns, points at him, and says, "You were a dog tailor, Tomas! You made pooch sweaters for Shih Tzus owned by old biddies in Bel Air!"

He points back at her, trembling. "I was a tailor and a good one! Now I'm an arms dealer. Things changed after the Reckoning. People changed too!"

He puts his hands over his heart, closes his eyes, and takes a big inhale, holds, and lets it out.

"Om Shanti," he recites. "Om. Shanti."

He opens his eyes and smiles, though it's uncertain. "Also, they were mostly pugs."

"Tomas," Eve says, "come in and sit down. Sarah, please make us all macchiatos the way Tomas likes them?"

Sarah rolls her eyes, and Eve mouths, "Please! Not for him, but for me!"

Sarah relents, firing up the Williams Sonoma espresso maker.

"Tomas," Eve says, "I have some bad news,"

His dark brown eyes get serious, and he sits down, and holding his feet.

Eve squats down in front of him, holds his hands, and says, "Clare is dead."

His eyes go wide, and he looks over to Sarah, who nods

in confirmation as she hands cups of espresso with just a little foam to him and Eve.

He starts to stutter and stops himself, collects his thoughts, and takes a quick sip.

"She was an angel—a literal angel. What on earth could have happened to her? Those nasty crocs?"

"No, dear," Eve responds, "we had one of our shindigs for the equestrians, you know, to pay the bills, and things got a little out of hand. One took a liking to me and wanted to take me home. He had an accident, and then his bodyguards, unfortunately, also had non-related yet equally fatal accidents."

Tomas's eyes get big, and Lilith can see little specks of gold inside the brown, giving them a three-dimensional radiance.

He mimics a kissing and spitting motion, exactly as Clare did that night, and Eve nods.

So zeks are an open secret at least here in the park.

"Did you bury her here?" he says, looking around and patting the earth.

"Cremated," Sarah says, frowning at him and nodding toward Main Street.

"Tomas, they killed her; left poisoned food knowing we were starving, and I got sick and recovered, but Clare was always so sensitive, and it was too much for her."

He puts his cup down and starts crying gently, more from melancholy than grief, it seems.

Big wet tears roll down both cheeks.

"All the good ones, the truly good ones, die, and the rest of us losers—present company excluded—go on living in this cursed world."

Eve holds his hands, nods, and gives him a hopeful smile, while Sarah rolls her eyes.

"You know," Tomas says," I was journaling this morning, and I had a revelation. This is the apocalypse. The A-POC-A-LYPSE!"

"Tomas, we need your help," Eve says. "We want to find who did this and get justice, not revenge. Find out who exactly was responsible and leave the rest alone."

"And cut their balls off," Sarah adds.

Tomas does a rolling motion to adjust himself.

"You don't need my help. Those cartel boys are all crazy about you and Clare—I mean, they were—but still, just put out a smoke signal and they'll come. Most would figure the ones missing were killed because of some kind of gambling debt, industrial espionage, or other shenanigans."

"We killed a patrician." Sarah says.

Tomas takes a deep breath and forgets to exhale as he looks around as if the air in the room might ignite.

"In that case, his cartel is going to want blood for blood. Or balls for balls or ovaries...anyways...you get the point. Might as well shoot yourself now and save everyone the hassle."

"It gets worse," Sarah says.

Tomas looks alert through his bifocals and takes another sip.

"There's a bit of confusion around the matter," Eve says. "But the patrician wasn't only a patrician, but *the* patrician: Emon Luxk."

Tomas looks terrified, clutching his cup with knees scrunched into his chest, and rocking to calm himself.

Then he looks confused, glancing around at all three of them, and starts to laugh a surprisingly big guffaw that fills the space.

He slaps his knees.

They all wait for the punchline as he takes another sip.

He audibly swallows while milking the moment.

"I just saw Luxk last week because he wanted a new coat of arms."

Lilith startles.

She thought the HIVE might have some secret spaceship to take her to Luna or Mars, but Luxk is hanging out in New Los Angeles, waiting for the Kali Yuga to end his life just like everyone else, and shopping for coats of arms on top of it all.

She is more than a little disappointed she won't go to space and that the HIVE's enemy number one is just as hapless as everyone else.

"Impossible," Sarah says. "I cut off his balls."

"Maybe you killed a different patrician?" Tomas says. "Or maybe someone who looked like him? An equestrian disguised as a patrician, though that's punishable by penalty of death."

"He did seem a bit off," Eve admits. "I mean, more off than the first time we met."

"He also had one of those cosmic scramble helmets on," Sarah says.

"Jesus, Joseph, and Kali," Tomas says. "Did you keep it?"

They look at him shocked.

He shrugs.

"Akron might be a shithole, but you gals are living in a veritable cave right now. Okay? And this is the Apocalypse. The A-POC-A-LYPSE!"

Tomas looks at each of them in turn, and they all nod.

"A reverse engineering team would pay an equestrian's villa worth of gold for that technology. They don't just scramble, but let you breathe underwater and in space. Who knows what else?"

"No, Tomas," Sarah says, "somehow, after the attempted rape and abduction of our sisters and the manslaughter—albeit in self-defense—of three human beings, we were not collecting trophies. Some equestrian must have run off with it."

"C'est dommage," Tomas says. "Regardless, I can help you out of respect for our dearly departed sister Clare, but also for a reasonable finder's fee; shall we say thirty-five percent of the spoils including all scramble tech and whatnot."

"Twenty-five percent of the loot and any scramble tech left over in the aftermath," Sarah says.

"Deal," Tomas says.

They all shake on it, his short hairy hands surprisingly soft and the only manicured pair Lilith had seen since Nate's.

"Tell them it's a going-out-of-business sale," Eve says.

Tomas pretends to take a note on his palm, "Princesses going out of business sale."

"Saturday night is a full Luna," Sarah says. "We start the show at sunset at the Mad Tea Party."

"And find me a new pair of accessories, my dear," Eve says. "I may need some extra help. And bring Athena too. I miss her."

"Done and done," Tomas rises and kisses Eve and then Lilith cheek to cheek, and he smells of rose water, nutmeg, and espresso.

He offers his hand to Sarah, who ignores it as she shows him the door. "Bye, ladies, bye Lil."

"Great!" Eve says. "This time we bring the curtain down."

"Did you notice he took all the espresso cups?" Sarah says.

"He's a compulsive collector," Eve says. "He literally can't help himself."

"Saturday night, the murderers of our sister Clare die," Sarah says. "I'll get the equestrians over to Alice in Splendourland and interrogate them there out of earshot, and Eve and Lilith, see if you can get Luxk to admit anything, even if you have to use your special talents."

"Word," Eve says.

Lilith has a terrible feeling that she's part of the San-San now and wonders who will be ejected or broken this time.

She has to focus on Luxk, get his W.Q. and seed, release him unharmed, and let Eve and Sarah do as they please.

Maybe, just maybe, she can fulfill her mission and include Eve in the next one too.

That night, Lilith discreetly returns to the bathroom where the painted rodent gleefully stares at her.

Is it judging her?

Shouldn't it be the one judged?

Isn't it the true autarch of this kingdom that sells fantasies and fetishes and pimps out Zeks to humans for thrills and stands by when they are cold bloodily murdered?

Lilith turns to the mirror, anticipating new missions even before they appear.

Both targets (#3 & 4) are Amirkhan Bio-Wep equestrians, and the Ten Brothers lines disappear even as she downloads the files and puts on sea green harem pants with a tank top and a matching blue headband with costume jewelry.

Nine Brothers.

Small Influences.

Then another line disappears from the top row to leave eight.

Holding Together.

So, the younger brothers, ambitious to start the Great War, are slaying the more cautious big brothers.

That means she is running out of time to complete her missions, and then what?

Can she still go back to the HIVE and live her life in her little blue cell alone after experiencing so much adventure, joy, and even love?

Or stay here in Amirkha till the bitter end when the waves wash over New Los Angeles, and entomb everyone in their wake?

Would Eve and Sarah even accept her after discovering she is the HIVE enemy and has been lying to them the whole time?

She has no good Ajas beyond succeeding in her next mission and being given enough time to figure it all out.

Then, all of a sudden, Lilith hears footsteps, and a figure appears behind her.

Lilith instinctively draws her tactical knife, which she hides behind her. She whips around to find Eve standing behind her.

"Where are you going dressed like that?" Eve says, standing in the doorway.

Lilith is stunned and stalls to hide the missions in the mirror.

Where did Eve come from, and how did she sneak up on her?

She was dead asleep when she got up to go to the bathroom.

Eve walks right up to her and takes her free hand in hers.

Lilith flips the knife so its blade is flush with her other hand's forearm wishing she could make it disappear.

"Why are you dressed as a princess? The party isn't for another night?"

She has to tell Eve enough of the truth to placate

her and reserve enough to not implicate her. She can tell her everything later when they are safe. Lilith kisses Eve gently on the lips, but Eve doesn't kiss her back.

"There's something I have to do. I can't tell you without putting you in danger, but it's important for me and will be over soon."

"I hate sneaking around and lies," Eve says.

"I'm not lying. I have to be discreet. Go to bed, my love, and we will both wake up together in the dawn of a new day."

Eve considers her carefully, must know she's going to meet an equestrian, and figures she just needs a little extra silver, so she nods and snuggles her cheek to Lilith's.

"Don't tarry, my dear," she says and kisses her again. "And don't let Sarah see you sneaking out. She's not as trusting as me and, as you know, is handy with that flamethrower."

Eve turns and saunters out with a kiss over her shoulder as she shuts the door behind her.

Lilith breathes out and puts the tactical knife back into her high heel.

She had almost stabbed her beloved out of paranoia.

The mirror is now empty except for her haunted reflection.

She wants to cry, knowing that she can trust Eve to

support her even when doing things she doesn't want to but has to do.

She feels guilty she has to lie to her and almost knifed her in her panic.

Maybe she can just come clean and tell her the truth?

Not now, not yet, soon, very soon.

After Luxk and the equestrian massacre, she tells herself she will tell her everything no matter what the consequences.

A true relationship can't be based on lies.

She meets the first target at the King Arthur Carousal, and he wants to do a big role-playing scene with him being Aladdin and her Jasmine.

He's even dressed the part, so excited he's spitting on her as he reads his lines written on lined notebook paper.

She just wants to get back to Eve, so she sedates him with Alprazolam, homeopathic lithium, and arouses him with enough Viagra to get the job done.

Riding him as he straddles a pink-ribboned jumper, she slips his W.Q. off using the edge of her high heel and leaves him asleep with his fez drooping over his eyes, hoping a Komodo doesn't chance upon him.

She changes into a gold bikini and ties her hair into a single braid for her next target, whom she meets at a spaceship attraction filled with fake space Zeks.

They fuck in the cockpit, and he keeps saying, "The

force is strong with you, young Skywalker, but you are no Jedi yet," whatever that means, so she shuts him up with a near-fatal dose of liquid nitrous oxide, halothane, and isoflurane.

She takes his W.Q. and puts it in her purse.

She skips the silver pieces the men gave her across the Finding Nemo Submarine Voyage pool, making ripples in the moonlight.

She is back in Eve's arms before the moon sets.

The next morning, the W.Q.s are gone.

**

A ripe Luna is partly hidden by clouds, casting a diffuse green light over the Mad Tea Party.

Sarah got the generator working, and they salvage enough gas from derelict cars in the parking lot to run the entire night.

The trees support a rope canopy with paper lanterns lit by candles that hang above the party guests, giving an air of heated intimacy.

Sarah found a record player and speakers and is playing Patsy Cline's "Leaving on Your Mind."

Sarah's dressed as Pocahontas again, and Lilith is dressed as a mermaid princess whose name she keeps forgetting, though under protest as she wanted to be Sleeping Beauty with the memory of Eve's kisses still on her lips.

She also dyed her hair red with henna, tied it in two short pigtails with turquoise bows, and used the leftover henna to paint eyes on her palms, the soles of her feet, and at her third eye.

"Baby girl," Eve says, after staying up sequinning her tail the entire night. "It's you."

Lilith is tempted to steal a kiss again, but Sarah is watching.

"Now, showtime!" Eve says, and squeezes Lilith's hand. "Remember, I can't live with myself if I bear his brood again, so you take Luxk's seed, and then we can escape together."

"I'll suck him dry," Lilith says.

"Break a leg too," Eve says.

"I'll break two," Lilith says.

Eve brings her into an alcove and hugs her, saying, "Love you, baby girl," and Lilith has the courage to say it back this time, savoring every word, "I love you too."

Lilith practices walking Bambi-like on her heels, with her butt tilted up to keep her huge tail off the floor.

She finds one of Nate's RNA pills stuck to the bottom of her purse and swallows it for good measure.

Eve leaves her Snow White outfit hanging in the bathroom and puts on a headdress she had crafted from deer, crane, and turtle bones with antlers on top from an African antelope that she gathered in the weeks since Clare's death.

A series of teeth from a jaguar she had gutted in Frontier Land a week before hang over her eyes and nose.

Her lips are painted with the same cat's blood, as well as three vertical lines on her cheeks and again on her chin in blood mixed with ochre.

She has on the pearl necklace Lilith gave her.

Beneath that, she wears a simple black skirt with a thin brass mesh top that accentuates her figure, and the men stop and stare as she leads Lilith—adjusting her faux seashell bra and tripping while trying to walk—through the crowd.

There is a mix of Amirkhan/Bio_Wep and Amirkhan/NAS_SPAC executives, and the D.F.H. flows as they pine for different princesses.

Lilith can't tell any of the men apart except that some talk about weapons while others talk about space.

Sarah insisted they all leave their lab-grown leather shoes at the door, so they move slowly, displaying pale veined feet, and are often shorter than the princesses standing in heels.

There are also dozens of pages bringing the equestrians drinks and hookahs or polishing their shoes while sitting, squatting, or standing in clumps like schoolgirls leaning forward and covering their mouths while they giggle and gossip.

They are all teenage boys, tall and thin with necks like swans and buttocks like pumpkins, their faces so pale they look bloodless, though their lips are cherry red.

Lilith asks if they are catamites, and Eve says that though they fill that role in a pinch, they are the precocious sons of BujiPetite hoping to rise to BujiVast that undergo unknown modifications making them beautiful, but also extremely sensitive, so their true purpose is to act like canaries in a coal mine.

Eve leaves to make the rounds of her regulars, with Lilith clutching her purse and standing in her veil of obscuring pheromones to control her agoraphobia.

Tomas saunters through the party in the same Toucan outfit, except with a sable jacket scented with musk and thigh-high velvet boots instead of flip flops, shaking hands, laughing with his head thrown back, and kissing cheeks.

He holds a pug in a rainbow-colored sweater and matching boots who looks up at everyone with a smile eerily similar to Tomas.

The pug's gold name tag says: ATHENA.

Lilith can make out Luxk spinning in a teacup with his two bodyguards as he looks around morosely, ignoring the half-dozen princesses who preen for his attention.

One leans on her friend as she slips off her lace panties and throws them at him, hitting him in the face.

He claws at them as if they were a spider, and his bodyguards rush in to grab them and return them to their rightful owner.

She accepts them with a grin, not bothering to slip them back on.

He is dressed plainly, even sloppily, in a real, and hence insanely expensive, black silk jacket that is too large for him over an **Occupy Europa** T-shirt and faded jeans that stop above the ankle, revealing thick bony feet.

There is the man that the HIVE wants dead or captured and would send a hundred Zeks to do so.

And Lilith has him in her sights, and honestly, he doesn't look all that impressive in person.

The photos in his file were grainy from before the Reckoning, and he hasn't aged at all, but going into space and being the only one to come back alive among millions must change you somehow?

"There you are, Lil!" Tomas says and kisses her cheek.

The pug smiles, and she smiles back and tries to pet her, but Tomas pulls away.

"Athena doesn't like strangers touching her," Tomas says.

"Jeez, Tomas. I thought we were friends," Lilith says.

"We are, dear. But Athena is not so easy to win over," Tomas replies.

He takes her hand in his and leads her through the crowd toward the teacups.

For such a diminutive man, he has undeniable presence as both equestrians and princesses make way, though he rarely reaches their shoulders.

"Good news, bad news. Then bad news, good news. Want the first good news first?" Tomas asks.

"Sure," Lilith says.

"Good news is that Emon Luxk is very much alive and here tonight against his misgivings thanks to my silver tongue," Tomas says.

"I know. What's the bad news?" Lilith asks.

"Bad news is he has a hard-on for Eve, and he's unwilling to accept you as a consolation prize. No offense," Tomas says.

"None taken," Lilith says, and gently adjusts her cheek, chin, and temple bones to mimic the waif type that Luxk prefers in general and in particular his first love who drowned in a boating accident on Lake Ontario when she was seventeen and he was nineteen.

"I can persuade him," Lilith says.

Tomas blinks at her and says, "Aren't you a tricky little minx?"

"Thanks," Lilith says and bats her eyelashes.

"Now, the second set of bad news. Promise you won't take it hard, Lil?" Tomas says.

"I promise I won't take it hard, Tomas," Lilith replies.

"Sarah killed Clare," Tomas says.

"Wait, what?" Lilith says.

She tries to break away, but Tomas's grip is surprisingly strong.

"You heard me," Tomas says. "Sarah poisoned the waffle mix to kill Clare and have Eve all for herself. Eve hates gluten-free shit but must have been starving. So her getting poisoned too was a mistake. You were a non-entity at that point, so Sarah didn't care if you lived or died."

Lilith feels like she's spinning as if she were a cup and the sky above a disc that stood still as she rotated, filled with nausea and then a clear cold rage.

She decides that though she is not a killer Zek, she will kill Sarah.

"That's insane," she says.

Tomas stops, turns to her, and smiles even wider with his eyes crinkling.

"Sweetie-Pie, this is the apocalypse. The A-POC-A-LYPSE!".

Lilith nods her head as if she needed someone to spell

that to her syllable by syllable.

"All the nice, sane people are dead by now. Just look at poor Clare!," Tomas continues.

He starts walking again, leading her on to Luxk.

"I have to tell Eve," Lilith says.

"Best not to. She's going to kill Sarah, and then Luxk escapes, and we both have missions to complete."

Tomas is right.

If she or Eve kills Sarah, then all hell will break loose, and Luxk will have his goons literally sweep Eve off her feet again and take her to his estate.

Then Lilith fails her mission and loses Eve for good.

Tomas is a stone-cold Go Master.

He plans multiple attacks and then only deploys them when he knows that no matter what his opponent does, at least one will succeed.

She looks around for Eve, who is nowhere to be seen.

Sarah is leading a party over to Alice in Splendourland; a group of pages holding hands, which is all wrong because there is no way they were here last time, so they are innocent.

Also, Sarah is no longer dressed as Pocahontas but is wearing her Artemis costume of white toga, Roman sandals, and a bow with a quiver full of arrows.

She also has Agamemnon's sword on a baldric on her back.

Two pages with name tags that say *Byrne* and *Brad* trot up to Tomas, and Byrne, his blond hair whisked up into a pompadour, whispers in his ear.

Athena nips at Brad's fingers, drawing blood when he tries to pet her.

He pulls back, squealing and sucking at his finger, then absent-mindedly runs it through his hair, staining it with a streak of red.

Tomas slaps Byrne so hard he falls to his knees crying.

"Excuse me, dear," Tomas says to Lilith, sotto voce. "Evidently if you want to extract a pair of limbs correctly, then you have to do it yourself."

He walks off briskly, leaving the two pages holding each other, with Brad comforting Byrne and handing him a handkerchief decorated with butterflies to wipe away his tears.

Lilith stands stunned near two men close enough to overhear their conversation.

They are dressed identically in slate skirt-like slacks, wool jackets with gnostic symbols overlaid in silver thread, and stiff blood-red collars.

They stand with their hands hidden inside their long sleeves, and each wear a bronze ceremonial knife at their hips, though the edges are dulled most likely to prevent them from hurting themselves.

Their jade name tags say: *Thomas Dee* and *Thomas Dunne*.

"Enjoying the ambient pussy tonight?" Dee says.

"It's not bad." Dunne says. "A little beat up, but that's to be expected."

They both chuckle.

"Talk about beat up.' Dee says, "Did I tell you I was at Mission Control when SolSymX went dark? Luna, Mars, Ceres, Makemake, Haumea, Eris, Titan, Io, Ganymede, Europa. Even the asteroid enclaves that were off book. Ten million people wiped out in a single day. Terrible return on investment."

He ogles a princess's cleavage as she passes by.

"I heard they killed themselves even before the Solar Flares took out the life support systems," Dunne says. "Couldn't take the cold darkness of eternity."

He says as he looks at a princess's butt as she leans over to tie her heels.

"It was HIVE sabotage," Dee says. "Some real Gog and Magog shit."

"Regardless," Dunne says. "There go our plans to save humanity by seeding the stars."

They laugh, though Lilith doesn't understand how that's funny and not tragic.

"I heard a rumor that two sex Zeks escaped into the oceans on Europa," Dee says. "Their owners fell in love with them and freed them before everything went dark."

"Great. Sea Monkeys in space," Dunne says, and they laugh again.

She checks her archives, and there's nothing on sea monkeys.

Some kind of first-gen Zek?

"Can you imagine falling in love with your sex Zek?" Dee says.

"That's like falling in love with your vibrator," Dunne replies.

She checks her face in her compact mirror and adjusts her makeup to a style popular the year, and season when Luxk's ex drowned.

New Mandarin script scrolls across the compact's tiny mirror:

Target 5-6: Thomas Dee & Thomas Dunne

Mission Objectives:

- **Retrieve W.Q.s**
- **Discern Amirkhan/NAS-SPAC's predilection toward further space exploration**
- **Release Targets Alive & Unharmed**

The Brothers chop only has seven lines.

Organized Discipline.

Then another line disappears from the top row, leaving only six.

Conflict.

Half the brothers are gone, leaving the most ferocious ones in power, and the fact that they are doubling down on missions and even leapfrogging targets means the timeline for the Great War has been pushed forward from years to months or even weeks.

Who knows?

Maybe even days.

Lilith honestly doesn't even care.

She's simply glad her missions will get her across the board quicker, even if that means there is no board at all by the end.

She and Eve can build a new one.

She turns to the two men and gives them her biggest smile.

"Gentlemen, pleasure to meet you; I'm Lil."

MAD HATTER

Lilith figures she is done using subtility with morons so doesn't even bother to scan their files as she uses the fat around her internal organs to double her breast and butt size.

They smile back at her uncertainly and stare at their feet like school boys who have been caught being bad.

"It's okay to look," she says, showing her cleavage, "but better to touch, and even better to suck."

She feels so top-heavy she would fall face forward onto the floor if her paper mache tail in the back didn't act as a counterweight.

She releases a fail-safe burst of dopamine, oxytocin, and serotonin into her bloodstream making her feel invincible.

She takes them both in hand to a corner where she stares into their eyes as she steps out of the outfit, leaving only her tail secured with garters.

They are already erect, but their eyes change from confusion to a cold, calculating desire to possess this beautiful young woman, seduce her, and dominate her.

Without a word, Lilith drops her top, and kneads her nipples to fullness.

"Miss," Dee stutters, "Lil?"

"Payment?" Dunne splutters, and she slaps one and then the other one hard.

"Your lucky day, fellows," she says, raising subharmonics an octave. "On the house."

They fall into a trance and thankfully get non-verbal.

They touch themselves and she nods as if giving them permission.

"Fuck the Gog and Magog out of me gentlemen," she intones at 100 Hz with a 200 Hz harmonic overtone in their left ears and then right, breathing enough pheromones on them to make a stallion kick the door off his stall waiting for his mare in heat.

She slips her outfit off, lays back, and splays her legs with her knees next to her ears and her stiletto heels touching the wall.

They take turns entering her, and she looks on blank-eyed, thinking about Eve as they climax again and again while she slaps their bottoms and faces.

Dunne finishes first and faints from the effort, curled

up in a ball like a child.

Dee continues rutting from behind as if his life depended on it, and when he finally finishes, a voice says, "Lil? It's Emon."

She turns to see Luxk is standing in his jeans, silk jacket, and **Free Europa** T-shirt with his still erect dick in his hand.

"What happened to Dee?" she says, understanding her mistake too late as she cranes her neck over to see Luxk still sitting in the teapot.

Another set of arms reaches out from the Dee Thing with six talons and pierces her sides, finding their mark just inside the ribs.

It raises her off the floor and headbutts her, breaking her nose.

"Cunt," it whispers as it injects a massive dose of Cyanobacterium into her organs.

Lilith instinctively counters by releasing an equally massive dose of Zosurabalpin and enough adrenaline to kill an elephant.

The Dee Dee Thing blocks Lilith from drawing her tactical knife by breaking her ankle with a heel stomp, gets an underhook in to control her torso, and extends its jaw with its mouth filled with thousands of tiny chitinous teeth blocked only by Fatima's necklace.

The gold bends and the turquoise chips with the pressure as Lilith bites her own arm to prevent screaming and drawing attention from the humans who would kill both of them as Zeks.

Lilith knees the Dee Thing in its still erect penis, and it loses its hold on her, so she drops to her knees with her right ankle splayed out at a ninety-degree angle, and her tactical knife ben.

She reaches up and draws the Dee Thing's ceremonial knife, stands with her ankle feeling like it's made of shards of glass, and stabs it right in the throat, then pushes the blade straight up into the Zek's brain stem.

The Dee Thing drops on top of her, and Lilith disengages her jaw and devours its face that's flickering from Dee to Luxk and finally a reptilian bird showing unfathomable fear.

Lilith fights the urge to continue feeding after she eats its eyes, resisting the temptation to consume the brain, reproductive organs, and marrow. But she can't help herself and devours its skull, brain, and pituitary, feeding until she is sated.

Dunne begins to stir, and she tears herself away, and kisses him, injecting him with a dose of Ambien mixed with Propranolol to help him forget.

Removes his W.Q. and puts it in her purse.

She wipes both herself and him as clean as possible, then leans him against the wall.

She slides over to the waterfall and showers, then carefully rearranges her face and outfit. Taking three deep breaths, she re-breaks her nose, uses her compact to check, and resets it as centered as possible.

She puts the ceremonial knife between her teeth as she snaps her ankle back into place with an audible "Snark!"

Leans back against the wall and releases ten grams of Valium, twenty milligrams of oxymorphone, and a gram of Ciprofloxacin.

She's glad she swallowed Nate's pick-me-up pills before the party, too, because the light in the room quickly settles into a nice powdery pattern and her wounds are already healing.

Lilith sinks to a squat and allows her figure to return to Luxk's preferred waif's form.

After a hundred breaths, her pulse returns to baseline.

What the fuck just happened?

Was the Dee Thing HIVE or Amirkhan?

Was it set as a trap for her, meant to protect Luxk, or was it targeting Luxk by taking Lilith's place, altering its appearance to match hers, and then stealing her costume to get past his guards?

For what purpose?

To kill her or Luxk or both.

Of course.

She has no time to consider all the possibilities before Tomas reappears so she drags the body out to where the Komodos will feed on it.

Tomas bee-lines through the crowd looking exactly the same except he now has splatters of blood on his cheeks and in his hair.

She covers the wounds in her ribs with a permeable membrane, closes the bleeding veins and arteries on her neck, reinforces her ankle, reassembles her skull, and releases short-acting benzos to stifle the pain as she reapplies her makeup.

She slowly manages to stand up and takes three deep breaths with her Po-Soul in her navel.

Tomas takes her in hand and leads her on toward the spinning teacups.

Athena, too, has droplets of blood across her rainbow sweater, and her boots are soaked in it.

"You okay Lil?" Tomas asks. "You look a little *peaked*. Perhaps you've been *ruminating* over that last piece of bad news? Heavy, huh?"

"Yes, Tomas, I've been ruminating and yes, it's heavy."

"Cool, so, the final good news is the R.N.A. cocktail you gave Eve saved her life, so she owes you a thank you."

"How do you know all this?" Lilith asks.

"I know plenty of things, Lil. For instance, despite official reports to the contrary, the Midwest is no longer a bland breadbasket, but has been an irradiated wasteland since the Civil Wars. So, if you're from Akron, Ohio, then you're either a time traveler or I'm the Queen of England."

Lilith pivots to the right, then spins around Tomas to run, but he meets her there effortlessly, as if they were dancing the Tango.

He takes her by the elbow none too gently and walks her forward Luxk.

"I even know about your HIVE mermaid shenanigans and honestly don't care. Maim and kill all the Equestrians you want on your own time. But tonight we're a team."

Lilith blasts every pheromone she has, hoping to arouse Tomas, distract him, and escape his grip.

Though she releases enough musk to make all the men close by erect, Tomas just smiles at her, his eyes crinkling through his granny bifocals.

"Adorkable, Lil," he says. "But save your parlor tricks for your marks. Now listen carefully: Luxk did die last time and is alive here this time too."

"Impossible," Lilith says.

The Elven Brothers—or Six Brothers now—had tried countless immortality schemes, and they always ended up dying from endemic cancer.

The InfoCorrectContext Brother had sought stem cell

treatment at WINhuB, to extend his life past the allotted one hundred year similar to the one that Lilith had given Nate, and the Others had sucked his stem cells out instead of gifting him theirs, and he was dead within a single night.

"Au contraire." Tomas says. "It's very possible though, of course, the original gets lost in the process at some point. He's been cloning himself for decades, long before the Reckoning, despite the Catholic Caliphate frowning on self-creation."

She knows Tomas's right.

The nine lives in Luxk's files could be best explained by him cloning a younger version of himself and the week overlap used to harvest all of its organs.

The three-month lacunas were when he died without a Khet ready, and his people had to sprint-breed one, and install his personality through nano-neural nets.

It's smart for him to clone himself before anyone else does and then kill the clone.

Khets instinctively loathe their Originals, and the HIVE fosters that antipathy by telling them that they are the Original and the Other has taken their place; exiling them to their little cell and starvation rations while their replacement is living their best life in their spacious home, playing with their kids on their lawn, and fucking their wife.

Once the Great War begins, their Khets are set free to assassinate the Original and conduct whatever sabotage the HIVE demands in payment for returning them to their rightful place.

Plus, the cyanide installed in their system guarantees their loyalty.

Still, even without all the Khet fuckery, powerful men are all full of schemes for world domination.

It's what makes them powerful.

"So? He's more Khet than man," Lilith says. "Let the new copy impregnate her too, as long as he doesn't kidnap or harm her."

Lilith and Eve can raise the baby and run away where even Luxk couldn't find them.

Deep into the prolehoods.

"I can see your mermaid brain spinning out clever possibilities, my dear. But hold on, because here's the final piece of bad news," Tomas says.

Tomas steps over a couple copulating and offers Lilith his hand to guide her over though her tail catches them both in the face making them wince, but rut even harder.

"Luxk has had some very specific CRISPR-MAX modifications he performed on himself since it's still technically illegal." Tomas says. "His seed contains guide RNA that targets a protein directly into his mate's DNA that permanently suppresses her X chromosomes, so she will only have his male offspring."

"So what?" Lilith says. "He gets only sons."

The Eleven, or Six Brothers now, each have eleven sons.

Had eleven sons, as they would have been Repurposed too—likely in front of them—to break them psychologically before a bullet in their skull broke them physically.

"Lilith, I know WINhuB doesn't graduate dummies. So, here's the clincher. Eve is—if you haven't figured it out yet—an Amirkhan sex and breeder Zek recruited from the inmate populations to be modified in return for her freedom after completing her missions."

Of course.

She was wearing an inmate uniform the entire time!

"And just because HIVE Zeks are either sex or killer or breeder; the Amirkhans would want as much utility as possible. More bang for their buck." says Tomas. "When the Reckoning crashed all the computer records, Eve escaped and ended up at the only home she ever knew, even if it was only from movies, t-shirts, and Saturday morning cartoons: here."

"Amirkhan Zeks arent' bred?" Lilith asks.

"That's a very holistic eastern approach, my dear, but here in Amirkha we believe in brute force reverse engineering; instead of breeding an animal to be a non-human being, we start with a human being and splice animal, insect, and even plant DNA into them along with bionic modifications."

Tomas pauses and squeezes her hand so hard it hurts

"Either way, you end up with something inhuman."

Lilith shudders.

It's true that she was bred to be a biological slave, but Eve was forced to become one with no other Ajas.

And once she found freedom and even love from Clare, Luxk wanted to use her for his own purposes.

Still, here was information Lilith could trade with the HIVE for her own freedom.

"Combine Luxk's super sperm with Eve's breeder status and she will birth an army of astronauts. Only problem is Eve will eventually, inevitably, die in endless childbirth."

"Why are you telling me this?" Lilith asks.

"Because if you can get Luxk's scramble helmet, it's worth more than an equestrian's villa—a hundred times that. We're talking a patrician's estate, and I'll share it with you. That should be enough for you to explore a career change, right?"

"Possible," she concedes.

"Also, we've already lost so much even before the Reckoning. Did you know they used the original score of Beethoven's 5th Symphony as toilet paper during the Culture Revolution? The 9th they made into a paper plane and set alight on *OK!Dokey!TikTokey!* Ming vases were used for target practice!" Tomas says.

Tomas stops and combs his hair back, getting control of himself.

Athena looks at him and he nuzzles her.

He lets go of Lilith, though she still feels in his grip; as if he has a force field.

"You're not a breeder?" Tomas asks.

She considers denying being a Zek at all and realizes he already knew the first time they met. He even knew her name without being told or anyone saying it.

Sneaky motherfucker.

So, she shakes her head.

"You can store his semen for your people to clone. That's plenty to exchange for your freedom. Maybe even some gold thrown in. You and Eve live happily ever after. The end."

He's proposing a textbook Capturing Race to get the winning stones first except in this case it's not stones, but RNA enhanced and stellar dynasty founding semen.

Same principle.

"Little hint on the approach, Lil," Tomas says. "You'll find this target less into small talk than your last."

"Who or what are you, Tomas?" Lilith asks.

"Whom, my dear."

"Fine, Tomas, whom are you? Amirkhan or HIVE? Human or Zek? Angel? Demon?" Lilith says.

"None of those things or perhaps all of them, Lil. I'm an Imagineer."

With that, and just as the clouds clear and Luna casts her brilliant turquoise light on everyone like a blessing, Tomas takes Lilith's hands in his like he's leading her in a waltz and box steps around everyone waiting in line to Luxk sitting in his teacup, guiding Lilith onto his lap.

Perfect opening Fuseki.

***

Luxk is startled enough to hold onto Lilith instead of pushing her off, and he signals his guards it's all clear.

The cups start spinning, and Luxk puts his hand around her waist to stop her from falling out.

She can see the faces of all the equestrians, princesses, and pages in the room and wonders how many of them are Zeks; perhaps all of them?

Luxk gently, but firmly, places Lilith to his side.

He nods to his guards, and they jump out and dislodge an equestrian and his princess from the teacup behind to take their seats.

When the equestrian protests, one boxes his ears while the other one kicks him behind his knees, buckling him to the floor where he cowers in the fetal position, covering his head from blows.

He's rescued by his friends, who bow deeply, apologizing for his dreadful lack of manners, while the princess wisely slips off.

There is a rodent head-shaped scramble helmet on the seat next to Luxk.

Lilith can't tell if it's the same person and helmet from the last party.

Luxk wears a short sword in a scabbard on his left hip. He has a frank and open expression looking out over thin chapped lips. His green eyes have a piercing quality she hasn't seen outside of Zeks, and even those were from a cohort who were deemed feral and Repurposed before all the Others.

He doesn't pay any attention to Lilith; instead, he's fixated on Tomas like a laser.

"My liege lord," Tomas says.

He kneels and kisses the gold ring on Luxk's outstretched hand that has a bas-relief of the solar system.

Tomas's eyes alight on the scramble helmet, and Luxk sees this and puts his splayed fingers to the titanium gleam of one of the ears and caresses it.

Lilith boosts her pheromones and begins her own Fuseki by preening her arms by her side, smiling ear to ear the way his first love did when they met on the quad before their Physics class.

He ignores her, so she doubles down on the pheromones and mimicry, and gets nothing.

Counter Atari as his first move, which shows he's a patrician and not an equestrian.

Still, she needs a way in; an Angle Play.

A Hane, bending his will to hers.

If not sex, then brains or nostalgia or even the desire to seed the universe in his own image.

Meanwhile, Tomas sets up his own play: "I am going to catch up with you around midnight with a new coat of arms I just harvested—guy was a real Adonis—but I wanted you to have an appetizer first: a real mermaid."

"What about Eve?" Luxk says, still not even looking at Lilith.

"I have it all arranged. A rendezvous with Eve just after midnight. She's actually wearing something a little more *Fin de Epoque* just for you."

"I don't care what she's wearing. I only care that it's actually her. Make sure you have a positive I.D.," Luxk says.

Lilith fumes; she knows he has a hard on for Eve, but he can have a hard on for her too.

Can't he?

Luxk drops a gold coin into Tomas's hand, who quickly pockets it and looks disappointed when there's not another.

"Yes, my lord," Tomas says and makes a deep bow while walking backwards until he turns and strides off whispering to Athena.

Lilith blasts the last of her pheromones, and Luxk looks over with a start, searching her face and his memory, and he shakes his head as if waking from a dream.

"I apologize," Luxk says. "So rude of me. Emon Reeve Luxk. And you are?"

"I'm Alice," she says, still flummoxed by everything Tomas had just told her.

"Like in Wonderland?" he asks, motioning his head to the ride next door.

"Sorry," Lilith says. "I meant, Axial."

Thinking she has the mermaid princess's name right.

"Charmed," Luxk says. "Prince Charming."

She laughs at his dad joke and lets her ankle slip next to his.

He doesn't object.

He signals his bodyguards, and one jumps out and sprints over to bring them a lit joint.

"Dragon Fly Hash?" she asks.

"Please…" Luxk says, taking a deep toke. "We're not *peasants*. This is a hybrid blend of genes from hash, opium, and queen bees. From my own private collection. Queen Bee Hash."

He hands Lilith the joint, and she takes a deep hit just as the ride starts moving with a jolt, and a jet of grey smoke rises from the generator.

Cline's contralto voice trails off and Sarah puts on a vinyl of haunting Moroccan melodies.

Lilith can decipher the lyrics from the little Arabic that Fatima taught her, with the woman singing about her lover who betrays her for her sister, and she swears revenge on both.

The smoke from the Q.B.H. curls up in her lungs, and she feels herself floating above the seat and not only able to sequence the light this time, but every face, hand gesture, and eye movement in the room, which brings her agoraphobia to panic levels.

An equestrian glances at his companion instead of the princess on his arm, indicating a same-sex predilection.

A couple copulates furiously in a corner, and when they finish, the princess doesn't even ask for payment.

Sarah is back from Alice in Splendourland, but the pages' shoes aren't by the door—they didn't return with her.

Which means they're all dead.

Lilith leans forward so Luxk can get a full view of his lost beloved's face.

She even shifts her eye color to aquamarine, reflecting the autumnal waters she perished in.

He stares at her but doesn't say anything or give away a single tell.

If he really is a clone and functioning as Luxk instead of just a decoy or an organ donor, then he must have had persona downloads spliced into his limbic system.

Though perhaps they omitted the romantic memories as superfluous.

Or he just got over the girl in one of his nine lives.

He must have had hundreds more in the meantime, though her tactical training taught her that the first love was always the weak spot.

Still, she needs more information to make a play.

"Tell me about yourself," she says.

Luxk gives her his complete undivided attention, and she basks in it, reflecting it back to him with her hands cupped under her chin.

"Not much to tell. I created SolSymX to save humanity from itself, and I think you heard what happened?"

He takes another toke as they spin.

"Not exactly a stunning success after lifetimes of work."

"I heard they killed themselves?" she says.

He winces, but that gossip is her only opening other than his obsessive desire to impregnate Eve with his infinite brood.

"That was for public consumption. Sounds more uplifting in some strange way; more individual agency. They actually murdered each other over everyday office banalities: differences in pay, perceived slights, who got the best views."

"I see," she says. "So Urth is all we have?"

"No," he says. "Urth is finished."

"Wait," she says, she says, as he hands her the joint and she takes a toke and says breathing out smoke. "Finished how??"

"Global warming is real, but so is the Younger Dryas Redux refreezing the poles and bringing glaciers back, dumping ice water into the Gulf Stream and holding the heat at bay, at least for now." She takes another deep toke and blows the smoke into his mouth with their lips almost touching before he continues. "As soon as it ends, the new glaciers will melt, and the continents will be overrun by the seas and not just with salt water, but with the beings that rule there."

She's bred from the sea but has never been there herself, and the HIVE taught her it's just empty space.

Now it's an avenging force for humanity's hubris?

And who are its rulers? Are they kin to her?

Is she kin to them and thus a harbinger of human kind's doom?

Lilith has never been this high in her life—nowhere near it—and his words fill her with true dread. But there's something else, something she can't quite put her finger on, thrilling every cell in her body: the desire to see all the works of humanity submerged in a heartbeat.

"The Kali Yuga isn't some metaphorical spiritual epiphany: it's a mass extinction event, a biotic catastrophe where one dominant life form replaces another even as the planet itself is recast."

He throws the roach into the crowd and a couple of princesses pick up and take the last hit together, faces beaming.

"People laugh at me, but I have good reason to want to get off back world. Keep watch on the seas, for when they rise, humanity will fall." he says

Holy shit.

Kami No Itte.

The Hand of God.

No more humans.

Doomed.

Hmmm…okay.

What about Zeks?

She can't ask that without giving herself away, but files it away for future conversation.

"So humans are over?"

"No," he says. "We still have the exoplanets. Human beings are just chimps a few million years ahead of the curve, right? Silly to think we can survive in space without some… adjustments."

So, Tomas was telling the truth.

Luxk wants to colonize the solar system with his own infinite offspring tweaked out on AI, CRISPR-Max fuckery, and space meth.

That's plenty for Objective Two, and he's fine, so Three is ticked off.

She just has to fuck him to get his W.Q. to fulfill Objective One.

Easy Peasy Japanesey.

Afterwards, she can simply tell Eve the truth about his insane plan, and she won't want to be biologically colonized by him.

Also, if Lilith can somehow get the rodent scramble helmet, then Tomas is happy too and will keep all her secrets and give her a pile of gold.

A Monkey Jump, sure, but the payoff is everything she wants.

Who knows what's possible?

If Amirkhans can make themselves practically immortal, they should be able to extract the cyanide from her system too.

Maybe she can really have it all.

Luxk lights another Queen Bee Joint, takes a really deep hit and exhales, the smoke forming a broken halo around his head.

"Bring in some other breeding stock," he finishes his thought.

He hands her the joint, and she takes a hit.

Wait.

What?

She needs to slow down on the Q.B.H.

Even her hands seem illuminated.

Is he talking about using Zeks to colonize space?

Oh shit.

Of course.

If Eve's breeding modifications are spliced at the DNA level, then all her children will inherit them too.

Though they will be all male, they will have her entire genetic library to draw upon.

"So, sea monkeys in space scenario," she says, as a joke she doesn't even understand the punch line, but it's all she has to go on.

Luxk startles and then takes a long look at her face again, seems about to say something, and then thinks twice.

Even playing footsie with him, he's still not erect.

As a sex Zek unable to arouse her target, her mission is pretty much doomed unless she can find another black hole in his psyche.

Information is information and seed is seed.

Seed is worth more than information.

Much more.

"No," he says. "Not sea monkeys, but more queen bee."

He doesn't seem to be talking to her, more to himself, but she recalls she has some queen bee genes in her too.

Her shamanic commissar never told her, but Fatima had stolen her file and shown Lilith before she disappeared.

"Know anyone who might fit that description?" Luxk asks.

Wait.

There's no way he knows she has queen bee genes, right?

Does he have a file on her?

No way to find out, and even if he does, the play is the same.

As for Eve, her tattoo tells the story.

Dragonfly genes, and that would explain the hinged jaw and consuming her mate, though not the disappearing eyes.

So that must have been artistic license by the gene coder.

Though dragonflies can lay thousands of eggs like queen bees, there is one important distinction between the two: bees don't eat their young.

Right then and there, she knows he's in for a world of shit with Eve.

Luxk leans forward and looks into his dead lover's eyes and says, "Did you know that bees live in total darkness in the hive? The queen commands all fifty thousand workers by pheromones and gets all her information from sensing the vibrations transmitted through the honeycomb."

Lilith knows this is a koan of sorts.

She met with her shamanic commissar once a lunar month for a debriefing consisting of a series of arcane questions that needed to be answered with an equally sublime answer, sometimes just raising a single finger or a cryptic smile.

But what will she win by answering?

The Aja of having sex with him and gaining his DNA for the Six Brothers so they gain mastery of the solar system?

Worth taking a risk.

A big risk.

Except spinning under the night sky where she can make out the Royal Stars guarding the vault of heaven, Lilith understands she's already failing the test.

Luxk continues watching her, "If you turn off the lights on them outside the hive, they fall to the ground totally docile."

She sees it!

If you were creating a Zek from a human baseline to colonize space, you would start by adding insect genes that can reproduce exponentially, and move in 3D and darkness.

They have a single supreme ruler, so they don't fight for control.

They may even be able to construct their own craft with extruded materials from their own bodies rather than try to traverse the universe in what is essentially a tin can.

"Can you imagine what we could achieve if we could unlock those abilities in ourselves?" Luxk asks.

"I can imagine," Lilith says, but she's thinking about Eve's question if she could fall and stay in love through all the madness.

Why conquer the universe when your own heart is empty?

"She also suppresses their ability to reproduce, and they accept it as their duty to the hive. The alpha queen bee emerges first. When her queen sisters are born, they emit a piping sound, and the first one born — the strongest — stings them through the wax even before they see daylight.

"Why do they pipe when they know it dooms them?" Lilith asks. "No one knows the answer or why she just doesn't...let them fly off and start their own hive or why they pipe back when it seals their doom."

The thought makes Lilith profoundly sad.

Why only one queen and thousands of sterile workers and a handful of drones for stud service?

Why not all queens?

Lilith uses her ankles to grasp Luxk's, and they balance each other on each side of the cup with their senses accentuated by the Q.B.H. enough to feel micro-movements of shear in the tensile strength of their fascia.

Even with their skin-to-skin connection, she can tell he's still limp.

She needs to play more aggressively, much more, before she loses him altogether.

She needs a Ladder Breaker to interrupt his momentum, his psychological scaffolding, and then, not right away, but slowly, ultimately bring him crashing down.

"The king has no sting," she says, something Fatima had said to her in passing, Lilith thought at the time as a joke, right before she strangled her shamanic commissar and WINhuB escaped.

"Pardon?" Luxk says, now the confused one.

"Male bees, drones, can't sting," she says. "They only have proto-penises full of spermatozoa."

He leans in enough that she can see his lips are chapped.

He says, "Right? The queen has sex with dozens of drones; she flies straight up into the sky, and only the strongest drones can reach her, and once they ejaculate, they drop dead back to earth with their internal organs out."

"What happens to the drones who can't catch her?" Lilith asks.

"The drones who fail to mate with the queen go back to the hive, and the female worker bees tear their wings off and push them out. It's called the Massacre of the Drones. Meanwhile, the queen returns to her hive and can choose which genes she wants to give birth to create a dynasty." He replies.

"Meet me in air," Lilith says, something else Fatima

had told her.

Fatima would read from some old timey poem through the cell walls at night when everyone else was asleep.

"Pardon?" Luxk says.

"We should meet in another life, me and you, we should meet in air." Lilith quotes.

"You have one baby," she continues to recite. "I have two. I should sit on a rock off Cornwall and comb my hair. I should wear tiger pants, I should have an affair. We should meet in another life, we should meet in air."

"What's it mean?" he asks.

"Most people think she's saying goodbye, but she's really telling her lover that she's a queen and he's merely a drone. They should meet one more time to mate, and he will fall to Urth dead while she goes on to mate with a dozen other drones and returns to her hive to start a new dynasty," Lilith explains.

"Yes," Luxk says, almost fevered. "Meet me in air!"

She scored a Karai, taking his territory in his mind and, hopefully soon, in his pants—funnier that way.

"Perhaps that new brood, the ones with certain adjustments, would survive the Kali Yuga?" she asks, pressing her advantage. "Either in space or here on Urth?"

He leans in and blows three smoke rings and she leans over and breathes them in.

She can barely feel her toes, fingers, or face anymore.

"Why limit your options to space when there's time?" he says.

"Time travel?" she asks.

Okay.

Now we're getting somewhere.

"How so, my dear?"

"We accelerate to ninety-nine percent the speed of light, slingshot around the Large Magellanic Cloud, and then return a year later in subjective time. A thousand years have passed in objective time, and the earth is cleansed by the Kali Yuga and we are the new Adam and Eve." He says, as if reciting a recipe for a cake.

"Wow," Lilith murmurs, struggling to say something more eloquent, and waving away the joint he offers her.

He's talking about time travel to sit out the Kali Yuga?

His ambition makes the Six Brothers look like the Six Babies.

This is Big Eye information where Four is Five, and Five is Eight, and Six is Twelve.

She reaches over and massages his now erect member.

Time travel makes him hard.

Who knew? Everyone has their secret kink.

He is about to say something when they are interrupted by fireworks that send men diving to the floor, covering their heads, thinking it's gunfire.

The princesses stay standing and cannot stifle a laugh at the men's expense.

His guards push themselves out of their tea cup and jog by their side as the ride slows.

Luxk tucks himself in, straightens his jacket, and puts on his game face.

Lilith reaches into her purse for her compact so she can see her own eyes and get a grip on reality. Maybe take her la Pulse, when her fingers alight on what at first she thinks is another D.F.H. joint Nate had stashed on her, but it's too big and hard and cold.

As Luxk confers with his guards, she peeks in the purse and sees a stainless steel artifact the size of a large pen, with script that says: **Amirkhan/Bio_Wep Modular Nuclear Weapon. Military Personnel Only.**

There are two markings at the end: one to adjust a minute timer and the other that says: **Scope: 1-10 kilotons.**

She nervously twists both settings, knowing she should put the entire thing down, but she feels compelled to hold its latent power.

Nate must have hidden it there so she would take the fall if the police searched them.

As the fireworks falter, the torches go out, and equestrians and princesses break off into nooks, disrobing, sometimes in pairs or threes or fours, and some just start copulating on the spot.

"I'm sorry, Alice," Luxk says as his guards clear a path through the crowd. "But I have to run. It's been a pleasure chatting, and make sure to look me up next time you're in town."

"Wait," she pleads, subharmonics all wrong in her desperation. "Fuck me first!"

She spreads her legs and grabs his crotch, but he gently pushes her off, closes her legs by bringing her knees together, and kisses her cheek.

"Raincheck, Lil," he says, and gets up and walks out of the tea cup with his guards trailing him.

Lilith feels a mad panic watching her sole hope for her new life walk away; the trauma from being attacked by the Dee Thing, hearing that Sara killed Clare, being toyed with and used by all these powerful men and women too.

A tooth falls out into her lap, and she kicks it away and tries to replace it, but for the first time, she can't.

She's reached her limits, and her hands tremble, and she starts to cry, weep really, not just for herself, but for the whole fucked up world.

She should just detonate the nuke and get it over with.

She puts her fingers on the triggers and turns just

enough to hear a click, and that's when Eve appears, pulling Luxk by his hand back to the tea cup.

MASSACRE OF THE DRONES

They tumble into the tea cup, and Eve climbs into Luxk's lap, wrapping her arms around his neck and nuzzling him as her hands slip to his erection.

The bones on Eve's mask make an unsettling tinkling noise and obscure her eyes and all her features except her cheekbones and strong chin.

Lilith tries to get Eve's attention to tell her about Sarah killing Clare, Luxk's infinite semen that will tear her apart, time traveling past the Kali Yuga, and the ticking tactical nuke in her Versace purse, but Eve ignores her with eyes only for Luxk.

Lilith holds up her purse and says, "Snow White? Want to go to the little girls' room with me to freshen up?"

Eve responds, "Thank you, dear, but I'm so fresh I'm ripe."

Lilith fumes, but Eve runs her palm up her thigh, and Lilith can't resist her touch.

"Miss me?" Eve asks Luxk, still massaging his erection.

In that moment, Lilith understands she's lost all Ajas.

If she ever truly had any to begin with.

"I believe it's the first time we've met," Luxk says.

Mesmerized by her beauty and scrutinizing the parts of her face he can see.

Luxk reaches in his pocket and takes out a pair of black pearl earrings that complement the white pearl necklace that Lilith gave her and extends them to Eve, who puts them on, smiling.

Tomas, that mother fucker.

He's helping Luxk pick out jewelry during the apocalypse.

He thinks of everything.

"Really?" Eve says. "We actually met twice, and you gave me a pearl necklace. Last month, I told you about our little surprise from the first month? How one baby became two?"

"You have one baby," Luxk says. "I have two."

"Yes, dear," Eve says. "Had. Past tense. You know anything about that?"

Luxk shakes his head, and both Eve and Lilith know

he's telling the truth.

Eve drops her mesh top as his eyes grow wide and then squirms out of her skirt.

"Well, my sire. I want another one."

She takes a big toke of the joint and hands it to Lilith, who sucks in its dark smoke, though she knows she's losing control of herself and the situation.

Eve leans over and releases Lilith's bra straps holding the plastic seashells together with her breasts popping out.

Eve drops to them, running her fingers, lips, and tongue over Lilith's now erect nipples.

The jaguar teeth tinkle as they scratch Lilith's soft skin.

Lilith falls into ecstasy, oblivious to Luxk as she phases out of his dead girlfriend's doppelganger and into the Lilith that met Nate and then the Lilith that stared in the mirror at O Ya Omakase and finally the Lilith who sat with her ear to her cell wall listening to Fatima talk about the Oasis.

She arches and invites Eve's touch with every cell on fire.

Eve draws her face to her, and there is a moment that seems set in time right before their lips connect.

Eve's skin tastes of blood, salt, and lime, and then their

tongues touch, wetness on wetness, firm and electrically alive, making her greedy for more, much, much more, as they fumble to free each other from their clothes.

Lilith does a big body roll to slip out of her tail but keeps her high heels on.

Eve's strong fingers glide along Lilith's jugular as she bites gently on her lips and then harder, drawing blood.

She drops her kisses to Lilith's neck, arms, and belly, then spreads her legs to reveal her sex.

Eve shoves her back in the seat roughly, and Lilith opens her legs wide, Eve licking and teasing her sex with her own ass in the air.

Lilith's spine arches as she's goaded to fullness, pushing Eve's head down with great gulping sighs and then with shuddering sobs.

Eve grabs her thighs and enters her with her tongue as confidently as if she owns the very flesh that reels from her touch.

Lilith cries unabashedly as Eve kisses her gently, almost as a child, and strokes her hair.

Eve says, "I love you," with a sweet kiss.

Lilith wants to say, "I love you too," and tell her about their chance — their only chance — to leave right now and not only the park but this whole world of deceit and destruction, power, vice, and madness.

"I'll always love you," Eve says, "No matter what."

The remark shocks Lilith.

She's saying goodbye.

Eve views Lilith as through a mirror darkly and smiles a terrible smile, reminding Lilith of Tomas's remark about them being inhuman.

She realizes that this was all part of Eve's plan, that her own plan to impersonate Luxk's lost love was banal and doomed, and she has lost everything, every desperate hope for love.

Eve has her and Luxk exactly where she wants them.

A queen bee with her worker bee and drone.

Eve crawls over to Luxk, who is practically foaming at the mouth with desire.

He sheds his jeans and reaches out awkwardly to kiss Eve with those chapped lips.

Eve drops to his member and expertly guides it back to tumescence.

She looks up at him and says, "Give me another baby," raising her voice until it's a scream. "To make up for the one I lost!"

"I'll give you a dozen," Luxk says, in a hypnotic state engineered by pleasure and pheromones and his dreams of ruling the stars as a king drone with his queen bee.

Lilith can feel herself sliding out of stasis again, with her bones, fascia, and skin melting into nothingness and then into the primal space.

Ultimately, the pleasure turns to pain as fierce as childbirth, causing her to shorten, thicken, and bloom so she doesn't even need to see herself to know she's now also Eve.

Offensive Mimicry.

Like a Venus Flytrap seducing its prey.

Eve and Luxk ignore Lilith as Eve gets off her knees and staggers to mount him, with the ride overclocking them in two Gs of gravity.

Lilith springs from the side, shoving Eve off the tea cup where she lands hard and tumbles in a heap, with her jaguar mask coming off revealing her hair slicked back and her mouth an "O" of surprise.

Luxk looks more than a little terrified, but Lilith takes her fingers and gently, but firmly, draws his eyes from Eve to her stunning blue eyes.

"Look at me," Lilith intones, using subharmonics based on his mother's and father's voices, all his grandfathers' whispers, and grandmothers' lullabies, a mix of all his girlfriends' moans during orgasms with the drowned one's cries as she sank under the waves.

"Only me."

She exposes her smooth thigh and turquoise garter,

rolls her pink tongue over her ruby lips, and touches her forehead to his.

His eyes cloud over, his body grows slack, and his erection pushes his pants out tent-like.

"Sleeping?" he mumbles. "Dream?"

"Yes," she chants.

He takes his hands and slips them under her shell bra, kneading her breasts, and she rewards him by making them a size bigger, with a sweet smile and her slim fingers around his erection.

"I knew you once," Luxk whispers.

"We're reunited," Lilith whispers back.

"I couldn't save you," he says.

"Save me now," she cries.

He slips out of his pants and she moves her panties to the side, bringing his sex to hers, wet, full of life, and endless promise.

She leans forward and kisses him, and he kisses her back, pushing his tongue into her mouth.

She lets him long enough to transfer Ditran, IT-290, and mescaline directly into his blood, lymph, and cerebrospinal fluid.

The combo creates a dreamlike state of arousal entraining his nervous system to hers.

"Fuck me," she whispers just loud enough to be heard above the din, her full lips promising release and so much more.

His eyes phase back to a trance and his body grows slack with his member hard.

"Fill me with babies. Forget that mermaid slut. Leave your college girlfriend to drown. Fuck me and only me and create your dynasty, my liege lord, my king of kings."

He pushes into Lilith as she rocks like the currents at the bottom of the ocean, so deep and rhythmic she could lull you to sleep with dreams only of pressure, darkness, and death.

They climax at the same time, and she takes in his seed with a spasm of gratitude, returning the favor with enough amino acids to build a baby of his own if he only knew how.

Driven by rage and the desire to be free, truly free, she mounts him again as her bones shift back to herself; her true self before becoming Eve, mimicking his lost love, her date with Nate, or even back in her blue cell learning to stand and walk upright and speak in air instead of water.

She reverts to the purest expression of her being when she first breached from the primordial soup with dozens of iridescent colors sparkling through her skin in the moonlight.

She kisses him with massive lips more like a sex organ and strokes his still erect member back to fruition with fingers closer to tentacles than digits.

He responds with a mix of awe, terror, and exhaustion, whispering, "Please *stop*."

Lilith phases back to her human form, with every bone and limb on the verge of breaking, covered in sweat, and with blood dripping from her nostrils, ears, and eyes.

She leans over and slips his W.Q. off his skull with her bare fingers like warm butter, and he slumps to the seat.

"You're not Eve," he says. "Who or what are you?"

"I'm not your queen," she says. "Nor your slave."

Lilith waits for the killing blow from his guards, but it never comes.

When she looks around, they are gone.

Luxk stares at her with fear and loathing as Sarah appears in the middle of the room, illuminated by a single torch.

The ride slowly stops, and there's a collective grumbling as couples dislodge from one another, trying to cover themselves as if in shame even in the flickering darkness.

Sarah holds her hands up for silence, and one of the space mandarins calls out, "Any old business before new business?"

Sarah smiles a supernova smile and says, enunciating every syllable, "Old business is every one of you motherfuckers has been found guilty of killing our beloved sister

Clare."

"New business is to pray to whatever fucked up gods you worship for your Po_Souls and consign yourselves to death," says Sarah.

A drunken equestrian with a beard and dark curly hair sitting with his princess claps his hands, and the others join in, creating a chorus.

"Bravo! Fine minstrelsy. Now, let us get back to the princess pussy we paid for."

He throws a copper coin at Sarah, and others mimic him until they rain down at her sandaled feet, sounding like a thundershower.

Sarah takes an arrow out of her quiver, lights the tip against the torch, and shoots it into the left socket of the drunk man, who grasps at it screaming as his princess crawls away and the men around him scramble to their feet.

They rush Sarah as she extinguishes the torch, cuts a single rope holding the canopy, and it falls, setting itself on fire and creating a blazing field of flames that ignite in crisscrossing patterns of brightness.

Lilith knows enough from being caught in nets not to struggle and lies down flat on the floor so the rope doesn't entangle her limbs.

Everyone else panics with one equestrian trying to stand.

He gets to his knees with his arms pushing up through

the rope like a soul trapped in hell.

Sarah takes aim and shoots an arrow into his heart, putting him out of his misery as his princess screams and tries to push his corpse away from her like it might infect her with death.

Luxk is caught in the knotting, still sitting upright and will be ripped apart if the ride starts unless he's consumed by flames first.

He can't reach for his sword or helmet.

Eve is nowhere to be seen.

Lilith waits until the flames in the net almost reaches her, then quickly throws it off and stands up on her high heels, avoiding the fire, burning flesh, and blood on the floor.

Sarah walks through the room, shooting men point blank in their faces, hearts, or groins.

The Moroccan music comes on again, the engine spurts grey smoke, and the tea cups start rattling, trying to draw forward.

Everyone trapped gives a big collective scream.

Luxk is pulled sideways with the rope across his neck, leaving a nasty burn, and strangling the air from his lungs.

Lilith considers letting him die: she has his sperm, Eve doesn't, and his plans for seeding the solar system would close all Ajas for her masters.

Then she remembers when she was choking to death and Eve and Clare saved her and also Rumi Axiom 950.

"If you wish for mercy for yourself, then show mercy to the weak."

Luxk has managed to catch on fire by pulling the rope toward himself, hoping perhaps to ease the tension.

She knows she should let him die.

But she's not a killer Zek, and even Khets have Po-Souls despite what the HIVE believes to the contrary, so she draws his tactical knife and uses it to cut him free.

She swats out the fire on his left side as he does the exact wrong thing, trying to shake it, feeding it more oxygen and reigniting the blaze.

Finally, she uses her tail to snuff the flames out and throws it behind her as it burns to bright flames and then ashes, lighting up their faces in its climax.

Sarah appears across the room for a single moment lit by a torch and mouths, "No!"

Luxk takes a dozen deep breaths.

Without a word, he pulls his scramble helmet on.

It seems to shrink as it wraps around his skull with an audible humming.

He scans the room, looking as if through the walls, and before the visor can fully cover his face, his lips draw back in a disgusted rictus of anger.

He grips Lilith by the wrist, and she realizes that freeing him was a huge mistake and that the Monkey Jump is on her once again.

"Come on, concubine," Luxk says. "You're no Eve, but you'll do."

Lilith struggles against his adamantine grip even as she formulates a new Axiom: *Have mercy on the weak, but not the strong nor cruel when they are weak.*

She knows all is lost unless Tomas shows up and saves her.

Or Sarah.

Or the HIVE.

Or she saves herself, but how is that possible with this trans-human monster manhandling her like a doll?

That's when the doors swing open from the outside with a bang.

There is a collective joyous shout of hope for their salvation, with the men thinking it's their pages or security forces or at the very least the New-LAPD.

Several run in that direction when an old male orangutan with flanges at his cheeks, grey hair to his shoulders, and deep sad eyes appears to survey the scene with melancholy grief.

He waves in a flood of Komodos and crocs that stream through the door in a feeding frenzy, oblivious to the flames and devouring men and women or sweeping them into the conflagration with their strong tails.

One croc catches an equestrian by the leg and spins him in a death roll, trampling others, and inciting the flames higher.

An equestrian stands on top of a tea cup while his princess curls up in a ball at his feet, and a crocodile knocks him off with a swing of its tail, breaking his back, and then turns and swallows the princess in a single bite, her screams coming from inside the animal's mouth.

Tomas appears walking over the fallen canopy, flames, and people, both dead and alive, in snowshoes stamped with R.E.I.

Athena, wearing a gas mask that covers her entire head, is in one hand and a titanium suitcase trailing vapor in the other.

Luxk sits down on the edge of a tea cup, ignoring the pleas for help on all sides.

Tomas kneels and kisses Luxk's ring.

"Help me, Tomas! Please," Lilith begs.

"You failed your mission, Lil."

"I'll give you his sperm! I have it. Lots of it!" Lilith pleads.

"I already have his sperm," Tomas says. "That was the trade we made for the coat of arms."

"If you don't save me," Lilith cries. "I'll die!"

"So, "Tomas says. "Then die."

Ruthless tailor.

Lilith dislocates her shoulder, twists like a corkscrew, frees herself from Luxk's grip, and bolts for the door.

Lilith gets three steps when she is enveloped by a rope net with interlocking magnets that twine around one another like snakes.

"Mother fucking Tomas," Lilith cries. "The bitch queen of the monkey jump!"

Luxk plants one foot on her sternum to hold her down while Tomas opens the suitcase.

She mistakes the contents for some type of land octopus, but it is, in fact, a *literal* coat of arms.

Six arms with six hands slowly come to life.

The fingers uncurl one by one, and the palms stretch left and right, up and down, as if trying to find a grip, the arms twitching and seeping what looks like antifreeze but is likely stem cells.

Luxk takes off his **Occupy Europa** shirt to reveal a torso strangely attenuated with symbols and mantras in some ancient script.

Tomas presses a sequence of symbols and recites a short mantra in what might be Mongolian.

Luxk's arms fall off, landing at Lilith's feet.

The ends are connected by living tissue like centipedes with hundreds of little nodes holding them in place but also sucking the life out of him.

The new arms attach to his ragged flesh, and there is a humming as if they are talking to his central nervous system.

He turns and stretches them into the air, the digits trembling in a strange but pleasing rhythm.

Luxk surveys the room and lifts his foot off Lilith just long enough for her to struggle to stand and feel free, before grabbing her again with an adamantine grip.

"I'm headed back to the castle if you need anything else," Tomas says, waving as he walks off over the ropes.

Athena looks over her shoulder at Lilith with dark brown eyes through the mask.

When a huge old Komodo lunges at him, he sticks his snowshoe in its craw.

The lizard tries to rip it off, but Tomas holds it at bay by shaking it left and right as Athena barks, and bares her teeth inside the mask with just her incisors showing.

Tomas is non-plussed as he uses the suitcase to hit the Komodo on the head, stunning it long enough to get away.

Lilith dies a little inside.

She has been so, so stupid underestimating these malevolent creatures.

Now both she and Eve are doomed.

Luxk opens her purse, missing the modular nuke in

his haste, takes his W.Q. from her, and inserts it back into the base of his skull.

He pulls out his sword, making his way through the crowd with Lilith in tow.

He uses his blade to spear a croc right down its throat and kicks an equestrian who reaches out to him for help.

When Lilith falls, he drags her by the hair through the throng, banging her against people, carcasses, and corpses.

Then she sees her: Eve, bruised and burnt, crawling toward the door up and over people, and past crocs and Komodos who ignore her, perhaps because the mask makes her look like one of them.

She is almost to the door when Luxk spots her too.

Lilith crawls faster to try to reach her first, but he's there in a few strides and grabs her with a free set of arms.

She tumbles along next to Lilith, who tries to bite his hand to free Eve if she can't free herself.

They are dragged together, their arms and legs intertwining, screaming and crying, and holding onto each other.

Eve puts her hand on the crook of Lilith's elbow in the most subtle and intimate gesture of trust amidst the carnage.

They are nearly out the door when Sarah appears

limping with her **Los Angeles Fire Department** flamethrower.

She raises it to Luxk, who scoffs and points his sword at her, as they both know if she fires, she will incinerate Eve and Lilith too.

Sarah pivots right to enflame a young male Komodo rushing into the melee.

Lilith reaches up to grasp Luxk's left hand and releases 108,000 nematocysts; each one containing a microscopic but potent harpoon of neurotoxins.

First, his left fingers, then his hand, and then his entire arm blister, swell, and bleed black blood.

Even with whatever AI, quantum computer, or neural web is running his nervous system at this point, he can't help but bend over with his hands on his knees and shit himself.

Eve crawls left, and Lilith right, just as the Komodo crashes into Luxk, with the gasoline congealing on its thick hide inundating him with flames.

Sarah holds out her hand and screams, "Come!" and they crawl over the burnt bodies of humans and lizards toward her.

They reach her after what seems like an eternity, and Sarah pulls them up.

They lie in her arms like a mother even though she is as exhausted as they are, shivering in every limb.

The canopy is almost burnt through, freeing men and women who are so crazed they fight the Komodos and crocs unarmed, kicking and biting like animals themselves.

The clouds cover Luna just as the fires simmer out.

Luxk lets his nearly skinned left arm drop off, and then another and another, the whole mass twisting and writhing in pain.

His visor reflects every face in the room, mouth and lips, and then eyes, before settling on Lilith.

The helmet emits a cascading series of pulses sounding like a mad war drum.

Eve covers her ears and screams, and Sarah stares at Luxk, unknowing but sensing doom.

All the fires in the room go out, and it's pitch dark.

Lilith screams, "Hide behind me!" as she exudes a single cell think veneer of ceramic over her skin just before the final apex electrical pulse emits at 100,000 volts — a hundred times what a seven-foot electric eel produces.

Every human, croc, and Komodo in the room twitches uncontrollably, giving away their position to Luxk's sonar.

Eve ducks behind Lilith, and Sarah behind her, who instinctively drops the metal flamethrower but is a split second too late dropping the bronze sword.

She is hit by lightning, losing her hearing and sight, and going into a seizure before luckily losing consciousness.

Lilith's vision strobe-light flashes at Mach speed, and all she can hear is a mechanical crackling siren.

Though she can't see, she feels the skin on her feet, hands, and face blister.

After what seems like eternity the charge lessens and Lilith slowly comes out of her wall of pain enough to open her eyes and slink to the floor.

Eve is trembling, curled in a ball, but at least her eyes are clear and open.

Lilith checks her for more serious damage, kissing her on her slick forehead before attending to Sarah.

Sarah lies with her arms and legs twisted, her skin burned from the fire and the shock.

She is covered by a dozen wounds and bites.

How she is alive at all is a miracle.

Lilith performs CPR to revive her and, having nothing to cover her with, uses her own body heated up a dozen degrees to warm her.

She unbinds Sarah's toga to keep it off the burns.

Her lower back has a Praying Mantis tattoo and on her shoulder: *Semper Fi!*

So, she is a Zek and was a marine during the Civil Wars!

Lilith has so many questions.

Who are you?

How did you really meet Eve and Clare?

Why were you trying to kill everybody?

She kisses Sarah's lips to transfer dexamethasone, norepinephrine, morphine, crystalloids and colloids, as well as the last of her stem cells.

The larger crocodiles recover first and turn on the remaining humans, easily overcoming their feeble attempts to resist.

Then they turn on the slowly recovering Komodos, slaying their cousins with cold-blooded efficacy.

Lilith needs to leave now, right now, or she is dead.

But not without her beloved: Eve.

Even if Eve tricked her to seduce Luxk, there must be an explanation, some scheme to capture his semen and sell it to Amirkhan dissidents or some genetic mafia: anyone who would pay enough gold to buy their freedom.

She pulls Eve to her and kisses her forehead.

"My love," Lilith says. "I'm sorry I pushed you off the tea cup. It was to save you! I was trying to tell you that Luxk will impregnate you again and again. To create an army to take over the world and then the solar system. You will die."

Eve regards her with tenderness, but the kind you have for a pet about to be put down.

You have already made the decision and tell yourself it's for the best for both of you; but in reality, it's just better for you.

"I know, baby girl," Eve says softly, leaning in to kiss her on the lips.

The gesture, meant to be comforting, only heightens Lilith's sense of disorientation.

"How?" Lilith's voice cracks as she pulls away, searching Eve's eyes for answers. "How could you have known?"

"He told me that my brood would rule the stars," Eve replies, her tone almost dreamlike.

"You lied to me," Lilith says, her voice trembling. "You said you couldn't bear his brood and live with yourself."

Lilith feels as if the ground beneath her has shifted, leaving her teetering on the edge of a precipice.

How could Eve not trust her with the truth?

"*You* lied to me, Lil," Eve says, her voice barely above a whisper, the betrayal evident in her eyes. "Everything you told me was a lie. You never told me you were a HIVE Zek, staying with us only to complete missions within the park, and even about wanting to fuck Luxk because he was your next target. Your ultimate prize for the HIVE."

Eve is right, but so, so wrong, Lilith only did all those things to stay close to her, to hope for a future together, to lover her and have her lover her in return even if the world is ending.

Eve reaches out, but Lilith flinches away, unable to bear the touch of someone who has hurt her so deeply even if she knows she is right.

Eve softens and kisses the back of her hand.

"And I didn't lie, Lil," Eve says. "You heard what you wanted to hear. I said: I couldn't bear his brood again and live with myself. I can't bear them and live, but I will bear them even if it kills me."

Lilith knows she has been playing Go like a merchant, only thinking about the profit of more life, and Eve has been playing like a warrior from the very start, accepting it's a game of both life and death.

And that sometimes death is the path to victory.

Still, she can't let go.

"Please don't leave me," Lilith pleads. "We can start over."

"No, Lil," Eve says. "*Everyone* needs to start over: Zeks and humans and Khets and whatever else is out there. There will be no Oasis unless we create one, but we need to clear the path first. Bring on the Kali Yuga!"

"No," Lilith says, pulling her to her and kissing her neck and cheeks and lips. "We can avoid it, head it off, sit it out in time, I don't know, someway, anyway. We can do it together! Escape or wait or create; whatever we need to do to live, love, and make a family."

Eve looks at her through a face so battered even her

eyelids are burnt off, lips cracked like old chalk, and several teeth broken, but she shakes her head and gives Lilith a brilliant sad smile.

"I don't want a family, Lil, I want a dynasty."

Lilith shakes her head, no, no, no, but Eve holds her still and says, "I love you, Lil," and kisses her. "But to our separate destinies we must go."

Eve stands, unsteady at first and then like a queen departing her court she walks out the door.

Lilith's thoughts are a whirlwind of the near impossibility of weaving all the timelines that brought them together — Nate being such an asshole, the police attacking them, surviving and being rescued by Eve and Clare, Clare dying, and Tomas entering the scene with his plot and Luxk having nine lives — it's as if they were brought together by forces greater than they can even discern and who knows what else they have planned for their puppets?

She remembers their shared laughter, the tender moments making love surrounded by cats rolling in catnip, and the plans they made together to survive and even thrive through the Kali Yuga.

The pain in her chest tightens, making it hard to breathe, as the reality of Eve's absence settles in and the knowledge she is never coming back.

She must go after her.

Convince her of their love.

Lilith stands to follow Eve when the sword comes down from behind chopping her right arm clean off.

QUEEN BEE

Luxk's bodyguard is covered in blood and his face filled with amphetamine-fueled rage.

He swirls the bloody blade and brings it down for the killing blow.

Lilith lets her rage surface—at Luxk, Tomas, her HIVE masters, and most of all, Eve—and unhinges her jaw, biting clean through his ankle.

The bodyguard screams and crawls away, leaving his still-twitching foot and trailing blood.

She lets him go, afraid she will stop to feed and die in the melee.

Tucking her right stump into her armpit, she squeezes, shunting stem cells to the wound, and cutting off the bleeding.

A Komodo spots Lilith and thrashes through the flames to devour her.

It gets distracted by the bodyguard's foot and then her liberated arm and Lilith feels a surreal surge of dread watching her limb being devoured bite by bite.

When Lilith turns to protect Sarah she's gone.

"She took the flame thrower and left Agamemnon's sword behind," Lilith mutters to herself.

The Komodo is almost done eating when it lunges forward and bites her other arm with its sulfuric breath seeping into every pore.

Lilith picks up the sword and stabs it in the left eye and then the right, blinding it and kicking it away so she can break free.

Before she can, Luxk appears, burned almost beyond recognition, with his sword raised for a killing blow.

Lilith tries to sting again but finds herself empty, so she does the only thing she can: she stands with Agamemnon's sword held in her one hand and uses her last ounce of energy to slash at his left thigh, exactly where her tactical training taught her to.

She cuts Luxk's femoral and the great saphenous veins, draining him of liters of blood in seconds.

She can make out his thin lips through the visor in an inhuman snarl.

Knowing that with all the AI, neural nets, and space meth, even that grievous wound won't be enough to kill him, she swings Agamemnon's sword high and true and cuts his head clean off at the neck before she falls to the floor in exhaustion.

An old mammoth crocodile slashes her way.

Before she can move, Luxk's head bounces into her lap.

She pushes the visor up to see Luxk's face with the eyes still roiling and lips twitching.

She puts her feet on the sides of the helmet, with the croc closing in, and with a sickening feeling, she shoves her hand inside his neck, grabbing gristle and bone.

She pulls out as she pushes with her feet to remove Luxk's head from the helmet with a sucking sound.

Remembering Eve's pigeon, she throws the head at the croc — but not before removing his W.Q., still pliable from all the orgasms before his demise.

The croc stops long enough to devour the head, cracking the skull until his brains spill out like Jell-O.

With the croc momentarily distracted by its snack, Lilith grabs her high heels, slipping them on.

She takes the helmet too, perhaps as a shield against crocs, and flees straight through the door, though the cries of the damned leave her heartbroken.

***

In the cold, clear night, a beam of blue energy from above hits the Matterhorn, setting it on fire as if by some adolescent pyromaniac and turning on the electricity.

The cars race around, spreading flames until they hit the final pool and extinguish themselves before crashing into a pile.

The peak spits molten plastic, covering its base and igniting trees throughout the park with huge drops of acidic artificial rain.

It's beautiful in its destruction, and Lilith takes in all its glory, grateful to be alive.

The loudspeaker spits out a garbled message: "*Our tea party is coming to an end.*"

"*Please remain seated until your tea cup stops and follow the signs to the nearest exit. Ta Ta!*"

Bloody footprints lead to Alice in Splendourland, and she has an instinctive sense of dread.

On closer look, she makes out Eve's barefoot tracks and Luxk's big bony feet's impressions, with the left side twisted and bloody and a single finger shorn with his solar system ring still on.

"But how could he still be alive?" Lilith wonders.

She picks up the finger, dislodges the gold ring, and slips it on her good hand just as the Matterhorn explodes in a riot of molten plastic lava.

She's Byo-Yomi, or counting seconds, before her only escape is closed, so she runs into Alice in Splendourland.

Eve is in there somewhere and also Luxk in whatever new incarnation he can muster, and now there are two queens who can't inhabit the same hive.

One always stings through the wax as the other one pipes for mercy.

The solidness of the helmet and ring on her finger give her a feeling of hope in the dark as she walks in and whispers, ""Meet me in air, my dear Eve."

***

Inside, dead pages stacked like cordwood block the entrance.

It's not clear if they were stabbed or poisoned or suffered some other form of debasement, but their lovely faces are unblemished and look to be sleeping in repose.

Deeper inside, it's pitch dark, filled with screams, cries, and growls.

She knows she will be dead within minutes of entering unless she can find a light source, and she's all out of algae.

An equestrian staggers toward her, using a princess as a human shield between him and a young croc.

The lizard crunches the woman's left thigh, squirting blood.

The equestrian uses his sword to cut off one front leg and then another, leaving the lizard thrashing but unable to steer.

He sees Lilith and, in a crazed fury, lashes out at her.

She stabs him with Agamemnon's sword catching him in the forearm, buying time.

He makes a lunge, and his blade slices the tip of her nose, spraying blood in her eyes.

To protect herself, she pulls on the still gory helmet.

Everything goes silent and still as it releases tendrils securing itself on her soft skull.

Luxk's gore and gristle seem to act as conductors because it flickers on for a split second before the whole helmet pulses blood red and then nothing, but darkness.

Lilith is trapped in titanium.

She instinctively knows the equestrian is in front of her, poised for a killing blow, and head-butts him in the nose, breaking it and bringing him to his knees.

The helmet flickers on for a moment, stunning her with its brightness, and then back to darkness.

She twists nervously Luxk's ring.

Nothing happens for what feels like a very long time.

Then she feels a current from her finger to her skull and searing pain as her mind comes online.

A single display in monk red illuminates the darkness:

Authorized User: Luxk 9.1

33/48/45 N 117/55/8 W

Urth, Sol System

It breathes pure oxygen into her lungs to combat the carbon dioxide, monoxide, and dioxin buildup.

Everything goes black again, and then every conceivable color lights up around her eyes like a peacock unfurling its tail.

The display comes up compounded with three hundred and sixty degree views in all directions.

It makes her so dizzy she has to close her eyes, but that does nothing to quell her nausea as she still receives the images through a neural link.

It sights the equestrian and outlines his movement lit in green as he stands to stagger forward with his bloody sword weaving circles in front of him.

The helmet emits tracking electric signals, but he advances even quicker.

Lilith steps back and falls over a page's corpse.

The helmet blasts him with 10,000 volts just as he kneels on Lilith's chest, crushing the breath from her.

He writhes back and falls over, twitching and burnt, screaming at the top of his lungs, but the helmet muffles it to a low hum.

Lilith lays panting as sonar, radar, and infrared emit from the helmet, reflecting the space in 3D with the page's dead bodies in grey and, hiding behind them, a pile of crocs lying in wait in red.

"Maybe I can use the helmet to find the Oasis?" Lilith wonders.

She whispers the word and nothing happens, so she spells it letter by letter, and the helmet buzzes for a very, very long time, scanning the planet and then the solar system, and comes up blank.

She recites Oasis in Arabic — *Wahatan* — and still nothing.

When she looks straight up, the stars are lit in green, silver, and gold with radio, gamma, and X-ray revealing their drift and making Lilith the center of the solar system.

A little lower tilt, and through security camera feeds, she can see the abandoned office parks, canals, and temples on Luna with the vast blue-green plankton farms still churning and turning the atmosphere fetid grey-green.

She looks a little higher, and the helmet plugs into cameras still operating on solar power on Mars, Ceres, Makemake, Haumea, Eris, Titan, Io, Ganymede, and Europa.

They show floating dead human bodies, still-living pets—cats, dogs, and even a ferret—and wilted potted plants tumbling through the corridors, with accusations, confessions, and dire warnings written on the walls, floors, and ceilings in fluorescent markers, fire retardant foam, and blood.

In the nest of stars at the heart of the galaxy, Lilith sees a massive black hole, its event horizon expanding to one day devour not only all space but time and even memory.

She looks down, and her vision is filled with enormous underground seas from the last ice age washing up against the Rocky Mountains and what at first appear to be dark spots hidden from view.

She adjusts the focus and realizes that the lacunas are caused by living beings nearly the size of the mountains as they swim, crawl, and climb, trying to find a way through the bedrock to get to the coast, their freedom, and mankind's doom.

"Kami No Itte," Lilith whispers. "The True Hand of God."

Lilith staggered to see the Kali Yuga unfolding in real-time, but not as shocked as when she looks inside herself and discovers all the human seed she has collected isn't sitting inert as she was told they would be by her shamanic commissar, but rippling white through clear ammonitic liquid and penetrating pink eggs arranged in long undulating ribbons forming dozens of wiggling zygotes.

She didn't even know she had a womb, and now she's a mother of dozens?

Jesus, Joseph, and Kali.

Either the HIVE was lying to her, again, or her own body, once out of their control, rebelled and demanded she be able to give not merely pleasure but life itself.

"I have to tell Eve!" she thinks. "We can create a dynasty together. But first, I have to find her, escape, and flee the park."

She drops her heart beat to one per minute, sets her skin temperature to match the air, masks her scent, and turns her skin pure black.

The crocs sense something is in the room and one hisses, and another barks, hoping to startle its prey.

Lilith stays cool and skates past them step by step.

Even with the helmet's suggesting steps and hand holds, it's hours before she makes it to the red queen's court, passing dozens of corpses on the way.

The bite on her arm is going into sepsis and aches so bad it makes her cry so she releases a small amount of short-acting painkillers and antibiotics to stay alert.

Her severed arm is better as she can just cut off the arteries, pull a membrane over the wound, and hope it doesn't kill her with infection or shock before she can rest and heal.

The helmet puts her chance of survival at twenty-five percent and even that is with brain damage.

She needs a Hekomi, or sinking down into the depths, just to survive.

She moves through the throngs of doomed souls, careful not to get involved, even though it breaks her heart.

One room holds dozens of dead and dying Equestrians, riddled with bites to their necks tossed carelessly aside.

She turns the corner and sees three princesses — the helmet identifies them as Mulan, Elsa, and Baille — holding each other frozen in fear when confronted by a huge male croc.

She shouldn't get involved.

Not jeopardize her own mission let alone survival.

But she can't help herself.

"Run! You stupid bitches!" Lilith screams, unable to deny her better nature.

Mulen bolts to Lilith who yells not to run *toward* her, but *away* from the croc; but as soon as Mulen passes its snout the croc bites her foot causing the princess to scream so loud it makes Lilith's neck hair stand up even with the helmet on.

The croc slowly ladder bites up Mulan's leg as she inches closer to Lilith's grabbing her feet for purchase and then the back of Lilith's ankles and then her knees and she gives her only hand, but too late.

Mulen is devoured in front of Lilith who amps the sonar up

as high as possible trying to stop the croc to no avail.

Elksa staggers forward, but watches as Mulen gets eaten for far too long and Lilith sees her odds for survival drop to the single digits.

Baille stands and pushes right off, but unfortunately, in the wrong direction and she too gets diminished hopes for survival even as she strikes an artful smile heading back into the darkness.

Lilith recalls from her tactical training when a death commando mentioned crocs have strong muscles to clamp down, but weak to open so grabs Mulan's bloodied cummerbund with her one arm to wrap around the croc's mouth as it pushes its snout into her calf in little viscous grunts.

Elksa staggers over just as the croc opens its mouth and Lilith cries out for help; telling her to stomp on its snout, but the princess steps right over it instead and out to safety with her survival rate skyrocketing.

"Cunt!" Lilith screams, and lets the croc go and runs as fast as she can in her high heels before slipping them off and carrying them.

***

Another hour, she is led back outside to a view of the *Matterhorn* now collapsing in on itself extinguishing its own blaze and covering the entire park with a layer of toxic smog.

Lightening illuminates the sky outlining dirigibles exchanging energy beams with the castle.

She takes the spectacle in with the helmet displays showing the intricacies of voltages and keeps the visor down to breathe without being poisoned.

Finally, she forces herself to go back inside the next section when the red queen screams: *Off with their heads!*

Lilith's hair stands up on the back of her hands and her heart rate increases with the taste of ashes in her mouth and she knows something is waiting for her around the next corner.

She looks at the display and nothing shows on any of the metrics, but she knows in her heart that it's her queen: Eve.

She takes a deep breath and tells herself to make a calm, cool, rational, case for them to leave together.

And not to be unnerved by Eve's charisma, beauty, and strong will.

She peaks around the corner with a piping noise building in her ears.

Eve floats with her dragonfly tattoo fully flexed across her back muscles sitting in stasis a meter off the floor in the lap of a headless Luxk who's burned flesh is peeling off as his left leg hangs limply from his torso.

Eve looks inhuman, as if her dragonfly genes have erupted into a riot of mutations previously hidden by her mask: she's molting, her paper-thin skin rippling, her eyes bulging into compounds, and tiny mandibles extending from her mouth, mimicking the upturned tilt of her once-human features.

She has four arms holding a bloody trident she must have scavenged from a museum, an even bloodier curved sword and the head of the Dee Thing with its face bit off, and the half shorn skull of Dunne, and a hookah filled with Q.B.H.

In that moment, Lilith understands, or thinks she understand Eve's plan, the difference between dragonflies and bees isn't only that they eat their young.

Dragonflies lay their eggs in water and not in a hive, their offspring live for years there surviving alone against all odds; growing, hunting, evolving, until they emerge into the air as apex predators.

Eve's offspring can survive under the waters of the Kalu Yuga, escape into the air once the waves recede, or travel to space or even hide out in time with Luxk.

She can't lose.

Eve is the ark.

Luxk's body undulates as if filled with nematodes, holding Eve in the air with his three right arms, her head thrown back in ecstasy and her red tongue out.

The display shows Lilith their internal union with his seed filling her womb, splitting and duplicating, and evolving so quickly that the zygotes are already developing rudimentary organs, proto-eyes, and even little beating hearts.

So, they are both mothers now and they only need to find a way to prevent being ripped apart by their legions of babies.

Target: Luxk 9.0 comes up on the screen with his torso outlined in blinking yellow and his still beating heart in red and: **Terminate to Maintain Chronological Baseline for Luxk 9.1 ?**

Y/N?

Lilith is tempted to use Luxk's own rodent space helmet to murder him, but she figures that headless he's harmless.

She toggles **No** as *This is all so curious!* barks from a loudspeaker.

She scoots back thinking she might have been spotted, but when she looks again the couple are continuing their cosmic embrace.

She checks her la Pulse which is dead center where her heart now resides giving her strength so she steps around the corner and lifts the visor.

"Eve!" she yells, taking every bit of her courage to face her lost love and this inhumane Luxk.

"Rally to me!"

Eve opens her eyes and tilts her head down to stare at Lilith.

Eve's face seems to soften, just for a moment, becoming as human as the first day they met, giving Lilith hope—just a glimmer, but that's all she needs.

"You have his seed and I have his seed and we are free to go!" Lilith tries to keep her voice steady, but starts crying.

Eve floats to the ground, dropping everything except the trident as she walks on top of her pretty toes.

Luxk drifts aimlessly as if he's a puppet with his strings cut.

He has bite marks on his forearms and ankles in a series of dark purple welts dripping blood to the floor.

Eve's strong fingers brush Lilith's hair as she whispers "*Lil*, love me my *Mer*."

She kisses Lilith through the liquid like visor and her lips tastes of salt, and lime, and seed, with Lilith kissing her back knowing this is all she ever wanted.

"My *Jaan*," Lilith says. "Come with me, we are both mothers now, our womb are ripe, and we can raise a family or even a dynasty. We can save the world together."

"That's impossible, *Lil*. You're sterile."

"I was," Lil says "Not now. Feel," and she takes her hand and puts it on her belly where there is a slight, but unmistakable pulsing sensation.

Lilith sees a terrible change in all of Eve's eyes, and

thinks it's because Luxk will try to stop them, but by the time she knows she's wrong, its already too late.

Eve wraps her legs around Lilith's, grabbing her one good arm, and they both stagger back to the wall.

Lilith tries to push her away, but her grip is like steel and Eve holds her sword arm so strongly it bleeds from her wounds.

"Eve, stop! You're killing me."

Eve raises her scimitar above her head holding it there as if passing judgment on Lilith for loving her.

Lilith snaps out of her shock knowing Eve is not only trying to kill her, but her brood too.

Making sure she and she alone is the ark.

Eve whispers in her ear: *Nothing ever truly goes away. The sun sets and the moon sets, but they're not gone.*

The helmet shows Lilith's chance of survival is in the single digits and rapidly dropping.

So, Lilith releases the last of her adrenaline, amphetamines, and even some black market accelerants derived from HIVE political prisoners' cadavers' pituitary glands.

She grabs the trident from Eve's grasp with her one arm and with no room between them uses her double jointed elbow to raise the trident behind her and stab her own back piercing through her breastplate, her newly formed heart, and to impale Eve to her.

Eve looks down at her broken heart, then back up at Lilith in total disbelief.

Dark maroon blood clouds her eyes, and her screams morph into a siren-like piping sound that makes Lilith fear she's slipping into madness.

Luxk's limbs tremble and then shake casting off blood as he spins.

He floats headless toward them as Eve pipes in Lilith's face, their blood mingling.

He lands awkwardly, leaning on his right leg, and, very slowly and painfully, pushes his back into Lilith, using his body to leverage Eve off the blades.

Eve drops to the floor on her side screaming like a banshee.

Lilith reaches behind her, grabs the trident, and pulls it out, shuddering with each sawing motion as her vision becomes clouded.

A final heroic tug and she is free with blood pouring out her wounds on both sides.

Luxk raises his sword and Lilith is terrified he will cut her head off just as she did his, but he brings the blade down on her finger with the ring separating it at the joint.

The helmet seems to gasp and then tightens further around her head with the displays going dark until she is starved for air and barely manages to push it off her ears ringing.

Luxk takes her finger off the ground, pulls the ring off, and places it on one of his right hands, picks up the helmet, and places it where his head once was.

He raises his sword when he looks down to her stomach and pauses for the briefest moment, lowering the sword, and she manages to sputter, "Your children. Let me live. Let them live."

He raises the blade again for a killing blow and Lilith flinches, when two crocs turn the corner and descend on Eve who raises her piping so high it fills the air that causes him to turn.

He picks up the trident and impales one of the crocs and his helmet blasts the other one with electricity before he turns to his newly bred bride and tries to save her rapidly dwindling life.

Lilith scrambles to her feet, sprints around the corner, past the Cheshire Cat's flashing smile and hears: *All of a sudden, I fall! Down. Down. Down.*

***

Lilith smashes through the double doors and out onto *Main Street* with Luna setting and the sun rising and casting rainbows through the smog.

The *Matterhorn* is still burning and she don't even bother to try not to breathe in the toxic smoke that blankets the park.

The Golden Horseless Carriage is on fire so her only means of escape is gone.

An energy beam strikes Alice in Splendourland, and it implodes instantly, sending up flames in every color of the rainbow.

The remaining walls melt into chemical bubbles that swirl in brilliant patterns, with the unsmiling caterpillar at the center, arms crossed.

Lilith listens for voices or screams and there is only the sound of the flames rising as the building crumbles into its sub-basements.

So, Eve and Luxk are dead.

Lilith wishes she could mourn the way Eve had mourned Clare; unabashed keening and the desire to annihilate herself in the flames, but all she feels is a cold, dull ache in the pit of her stomach.

She realizes that Eve never loved her, was merely toying with her to get closer to Luxk and steal his seed, to take over as the Urth's queen bee and genetic ark that will survive the Kali Yuga and seed the new world to come at the Oasis.

She collapses into a fetal ball holding her hand to her wounds to try to stop from bleeding out.

She thinks she hears a piping sound from the distance and when she puts her ear to the ground she is sure that her mind is playing tricks on her.

She should just accept death.

Why run from it anymore?

She starts to lose the light and knows she's ready to die.

The helmet must have installed ambient AI in her nervous system because she can still see the Milky Way swirl though it is now daylight though dark as night from all the smoke.

Lilith fishes the nuke out of her purse, listens to it ticking, and then twists both ends to max, and presses the trigger.

The sky is filled with Senate Syndicate dirigibles, and the castle, now repaired, has its spire painted blue and gold, reaching toward the heavens, sparkling with lights in all its glory, just as it was in the days of old.

ABOUT THE AUTHOR

Wine Lo Borgias

I am what Thais would call a *Kathoey* or Ladyboy since I was born in a boy's body, but felt like a girl even at a young age and my farmer parents in Isan let me dress as a girl until I reached puberty and then realized it wasn't a phase and kicked me out of the house at fourteen.

I begged for money on the side of the road and a kind monk gave me bus fare to Bangkok and enough extra to pay a week's rent and feed myself for a day. I got a cheap room with a mattress with no windows under the Skytrain and could only sleep from midnight to six am when it didn't run though I could still hear drunks screaming outside.

I sold incense on the street and started teaching myself English talking with tourists and by reading an old dog-eared copy of Thoreau's *Walden*. I didn't understand most of the words so would look them up and his description of life in 19th century pastoral America seemed like a fairy tale as I sat on the street corner reading by street light in Krungthep: the City of Angels.

When I turned seventeen, I became a bar girl and over the next ten years and often aty the same time was a taxi driver, plumber (self-taught), Muay Thai fighter and instructor (8-2), visual artist and Grab driver. I was also briefly addicted to ya ba (smokable speed) while a bar girl, Grab driver, and visual artist making anon graffiti throughout Bangkok.

I often had to deal with aggressive men who were a lot bigger than I am and I had to think on my feet just to survive, but still, several times bad things happened and talking to other girls I realized I was not alone. Some of those experiences from being a bar girl, both good and bad, inform the life of the *zek* characters in Lilith

My American boyfriend helped me get clean and sober with the help of N.A. and I started writing short stories based on people I met in Bangkok including clients, madams, police, boyfriends and girlfriends, and even the psychiatrists I met both as clients and my therapists.

As a bar girl, I noticed that both the Americans and Chinese men (some who were high raking officials) were obsessed with each other, the strengths and weaknesses of their cultures, and the coming conflict between their countries.

I got to thinking about how ordinary, everyday people get caught up in historical events when they are often just looking to get through the day or night (i.e. complete their mission), find friendship, family and meaning, and sometimes against all odds: love.

I hope you enjoy *Lilith*.

I put my heart and soul into it to try to connect with other people I will never meet in real life, but am connected to by the heart.

Yin Di.

Lo.

www.ingramcontent.com/pod-product-compliance
Ingram Content Group UK Ltd.
Pitfield, Milton Keynes, MK11 3LW, UK
UKHW031022060125
452819UK00019B/41